Thumbprint Mysteries

CHAMPAGNE AT RISK

BY

JOAN LOWERY NIXON
AND
KATHLEEN NIXON BRUSH

CB

CONTEMPORARY BOOKS

a division of NTC/CONTEMPORARY PUBLISHING GROUP
Lincolnwood, Illinois USA

Thumbprint
Mysteries

MORE THUMBPRINT MYSTERIES

by Joan Lowery Nixon
and Kathleen Nixon Brush:

Champagne at the Murder
Champagne with a Corpse

This is a work of fiction. The characters, incidents, and dialogues are products of the author's imagination and are not to be construed as real. Any resemblance to actual events or persons, living or dead, is entirely coincidental.

Cover Illustration: Tim Spransey

ISBN: 0-8092-0671-4

Published by Contemporary Books,
a division of NTC/Contemporary Publishing Group, Inc.,
4255 West Touhy Avenue,
Lincolnwood (Chicago), Illinois 60646-1975 U.S.A.
© 1998 Joan Lowery Nixon and Kathleen Nixon Brush
Manufactured in the United States of America.

890 QB 0987654321

CHAPTER 1

I took a quick breath as I gazed out the front windows of our family's Silver Ridge Hotel. Before me lay pine- and spruce-covered mountains dotted with golden aspens. The beauty of this quiet, Colorado mountain town never failed to move me.

My trim, slender grandmother stepped up beside me. "Stacy, look at that clear, blue sky," she said. "It will be a perfect day for the writers."

Her voice was filled with excitement. Gran loves to read—especially mysteries. And all of the writers who were coming to Silver Ridge were authors of best-selling mystery novels. At the moment, my grandmother sparkled like a stagestruck teenager in a fan club. Gran looked at her watch and gave a little jump. "They'll be here any minute."

I just smiled. Gran was thrilled that we were going to have a group of well-known, published mystery writers as guests at the hotel. I wasn't going to spoil the weekend for her by telling her what I had found out about the writers.

Prescott Publishing, which is based in Colorado, has made a name for itself with its list of best-selling mystery authors. And each year Prescott invites its writers whose books have the highest number of sales to a hotel for a special weekend retreat. During the retreat they are honored at a small, private award dinner. This year Prescott had chosen our hotel in Silver Ridge and had reserved seven rooms.

Gran looked wistful as she said, "Stacy, I've been hoping that after the writers see what a wonderful hotel we have, at least one of them will use it as a setting in a book. Wouldn't that be great publicity?"

"Yes," I answered. I knew how much she missed the local items that used to run in our town's weekly newspaper. Someone had bought Barry Harrison's print shop, but rumors were that the new owner wouldn't put out a newspaper.

Gran was sure that everything would run smoothly this weekend. I couldn't bring myself to tell her that if we weren't very careful, Prescott Publishing could bring us the wrong kind of publicity. Since I was Chief of Security for the hotel, it would be up to me to make sure that didn't happen.

"Amy Prescott has been so lovely to deal with," Gran said. "I'm eager to meet her in person. She told me all about the writers so we'd know what kind of special attention they'd need."

"She told you everything?" I was startled.

"Oh, yes," Gran said. She began ticking items off on her fingers. "Duncan Tyler can be a bit grumpy in the mornings. Clara Vine loves to have chocolates left on her pillow each evening. That's chocolates—plural. One's never enough. Greg and Ginger Gage still act like honeymooners, although they've been married for almost ten years. Lady Jane Hampton insists on being served high tea at four o'clock each afternoon. And Mark Bannon flirts with all the women." She giggled again. "I've seen his photograph on his book jackets. He's very handsome." She stopped speaking and smiled.

"That's it?" I asked. "That's all she told you?"

"Oh, there were a few other little things. I wrote them down so I wouldn't forget," Gran said. "One of the writers doesn't like fish, and one is allergic to grapefruit. Little things like that."

I didn't tell Gran what I was thinking. It was clear that Amy Prescott hadn't told Gran everything. She hadn't told Gran about the crime that happened last year. She hadn't told her about the theft.

I take my job as Chief of Security seriously. So when I found that the Prescott mystery writers were coming to Silver Ridge, I did what I always do when we get requests for reservations from any convention or group. I checked to make sure their reservations could be honored. Through a routine search I was surprised to find that at the previous year's Prescott writers' retreat in Boulder, Colorado, the award check had been stolen.

Each year Prescott Publishing gives a five-thousand-dollar bonus check to the mystery writer whose books had the highest sales figures during the past year. After each dinner Amy Prescott gives a short speech. Then she hands an envelope containing the bonus check to the winning author.

But last year something strange had happened. The winning author—Duncan Tyler—eagerly tore open the envelope and found it to be empty. The check had been stolen and was cashed the next day. The crime had never been solved.

Nothing like that is going to happen here at Silver Ridge, I promised myself.

My uncle Jim strode into the lobby. "There you are," he called. He held up a book as he hurried toward us. "Look at this photo!" he said.

Gran nodded. "That's Clara Vine," she told him.

"Isn't she something?" Uncle Jim boomed. At six feet, six inches, he has a voice to match his size. "I bought this book at O'Connor's store so I can ask her to sign it," he said.

"It's not really your kind of book," Gran said. "It's a romantic suspense novel. I don't think you'll be interested in it."

Uncle Jim's grin was teasing. "Romance is exactly what I'm interested in," he said.

Gran didn't bother to answer. Everyone in Silver Ridge knew that Jim was constantly falling in and out of love. Gran looked at her watch again and said, "The writers will be here soon."

"About the writers. You told me to plan some activities for them, so I did," Uncle Jim said. "They'll start with an early morning hike tomorrow before breakfast. We'll pack coffee and donuts, and I should have them back in time for a late lunch. After lunch we can go by van to a valley where we're bound to see a herd of elk. And in the evening I'll put up the telescope at the rangers' hut and let them look at the stars. I'm counting on showing them a good view of Saturn."

Uncle Jim is definitely an outdoors person. I doubted that the writers would share this all-day-and-evening love of the great outdoors.

"You might have to change some of your schedule," I told him. "Remember that the most interesting event for the writers will be the award dinner tonight."

Even though I didn't mean to sound sharp, I did. Maybe it was because of my worry about that award bonus check. Uncle Jim looked surprised. He put a hand on my shoulder and asked, "What's bothering you, Stacy? You seem stressed out about this weekend."

Gran was studying me, so I couldn't give Uncle Jim a straight answer. "Sorry. I didn't mean to sound so cross," I answered. "I'd like everything about this weekend to go smoothly. Since I'm in charge of security, I don't want to run into any unexpected problems."

Uncle Jim laughed. "Problems? With a handful of harmless writers?" He tried to look serious as he said, "I'll keep them too busy to get into trouble. I may even take them fishing."

He put his arm around Gran's shoulders. "Show me where you want those flats of yellow mums planted," he said. "The gardeners have been asking me."

As Gran and Uncle Jim left the lobby, Dad came to join me. He looked unhappy as he said, "Deputy Ramon Gonzales told me you hired him to guard the hotel safe this weekend. Why didn't you consult me before you offered him a job?"

I was so surprised that I spoke bluntly without thinking. "I didn't know that I had to go over every decision with you. I arranged for help in guarding the award check. Making a security decision is a normal part of this job."

Dad cleared his throat. I could see him make the effort to sound less formal and businesslike. I know it's hard for Dad to unbend, but I couldn't shake the feeling that I was ten years old and being scolded. "Before you hire even temporary help, I expect you to check it out with me. You should ask if we have the money available or what forms need to be filled in. Things like that."

I fought back my hurt and anger. I couldn't see why my father wanted to make such a fuss over something so simple. "I only arranged for Ramon to be here during the weekend," I said. "That shouldn't require spending a lot of money or filling out forms. He does have a full-time job with the county."

Dad sighed. "Stacy, ever since you began working here four months ago, you've been acting as if you alone can handle any problem. You never talk over what you're doing with the rest of us. You make quick decisions and act upon them."

"What decisions?" I blurted out. "Like installing a handrail on the ramp to the back door? Or posting the altitude on the trail that leads into the mountain behind the hotel? You know some of our elderly guests might—"

"Never mind reciting a list, Stacy," Dad said. "I think I've made my point. We're a family. I'd like us all to work together as a team." Before he turned to walk away he said, "Teamwork. That's the key. That's what I want you to keep in mind."

As Dad walked back to his office, I shook my head. I'd never been able to really please him, no matter how hard I tried. But this job at Silver Ridge meant a lot to me. When Dad, Gran, and Uncle Jim asked me to leave my job in Denver and take on the post of Chief of Security here at our family hotel, I was glad to accept. I love my family. I wanted to be a part of their lives. I wanted them to need me.

I was here now, and I planned to stay. I was going to do the best I could at my job. That's all any of them could ask.

I saw Ramon come out of Dad's office, so I eagerly went to meet him.

Ramon was wearing a navy blue suit instead of his beige deputy sheriff uniform. I liked the way he looked in a suit and tie. Of course, I liked the way he looked in a uniform too. To be honest, I always liked the way he looked. Ramon is tall with dark hair and a trim mustache. When he smiles, I think he's the best-looking guy I've ever seen.

Ramon gave me a hug. Then he stepped away to show that it was time to talk business. "I asked the police in Boulder for their report on the Prescott theft last year," he told me. "I can give you some details now." He handed me a file folder with several sheets of paper in it.

Keisha turned from the front desk to wink at me as we passed.

"Business," I mouthed at her. Then I smiled. It was no secret around Silver Ridge how Ramon and I felt about each other.

As we walked back to my office, I looked over the report. Once at my desk, I read the report eagerly. Then I put it down and looked at Ramon, who had made himself comfortable in one of the guest chairs.

"This doesn't really answer my questions," I told him. "Let's go over the facts. Last year Amy Prescott brought an envelope with the five-thousand-dollar award check in it to the hotel in Boulder. She asked to keep the check in the hotel safe until time for their award dinner. Before the dinner she asked for the envelope. Then she put the envelope into her briefcase and kept the briefcase next to her chair during the meal. The story in the Boulder newspaper said that she hadn't left her chair. The briefcase was never out of her sight. After dinner was over, Amy Prescott gave a short speech praising all the writers in the group. Then she gave the envelope to the writer who had sold the most books that year—Duncan

Tyler. Mr. Tyler thanked her and opened the envelope. It contained a blank piece of paper."

"Okay. Those are the facts. What are your questions?" Ramon asked.

"First question," I said. "Did the police find any fingerprints on the envelope?"

"Only one clear one, and that was Amy's. But there were other prints that had been smudged," Ramon said.

I looked back at the report he had given to me. "The check had been cashed the following morning at a large and busy bank in Boulder. It just happens that was the bank where Duncan Tyler had a savings account."

"There was nothing to link the person who cashed the check to Tyler," Ramon said. "It's a good-sized bank, and they do a great deal of Saturday morning business. The teller who cashed the check couldn't remember who had brought the check into the bank. The name signed on the check was not in Tyler's handwriting."

"I'm puzzled about something," I told Ramon. "Did the thief know that Duncan Tyler had a savings account in that bank?"

"Only one person admitted to knowing," Ramon said. "The publisher's granddaughter—Amy Prescott."

CHAPTER 2

Gran gave a quick knock at my office door, opened it, and took an excited hop inside the room. "The van from Prescott Publishing just drove up!" she said.

I left the report on my desk and followed Gran out to the drive to greet the authors. The head bellman, Lew Parker, was right behind us with his luggage cart.

"Prescott Publishing" was painted across the side of the large, beige van. It looked very expensive. It was exactly the right coach for royalty—or for famous authors. As the side door slid open, I took a deep breath like a runner just before the starting gun. The weekend was beginning.

An African-American woman about my age—late twenties or early thirties—stepped out of the van on the driver's side. She strode briskly around the front of the van to the side door and held out a hand to help the writers climb out.

"That's Amy Prescott," Gran whispered to me. "Don't you love that beige suede pantsuit she's wearing?"

I nodded and tried not to think of what Ramon had just told me. The police had found no proof that Amy had been guilty of the theft, and I was glad. I saw the warmth in her eyes as she smiled, and I liked her immediately. I watched the writers who were climbing from the van. I recognized the first writer as Greg Gage. He waved away Amy's helping hand and jumped from the van. I knew that Greg co-authored books with his wife, Ginger. *The Fifth Star* was their most recent book.

Although I had intended to read at least one book written by each author, I hadn't finished *The Fifth Star* yet. It was about a young couple who were supposed to be protecting a famous movie star whose life was in danger. I wasn't sure which of the other characters were actually threatening the movie star, because the mystery didn't seem important to the authors. Most of the plot had to do with the young couple's love story.

Greg turned and held out his hand to help his wife down the step from the van. She was dressed in a filmy, flowered print dress, and her long, blond hair floated around her face.

Greg and Ginger held hands as they walked up the steps to the hotel. They didn't stop to look at the beautiful scenery. They didn't stop when Gran said, "Welcome to the Silver Ridge Hotel." Ginger raised one hand and wiggled her fingers in a wave, but they had eyes only for each other.

The next passenger from the van was a small, plump woman with curly gray hair. She wore sturdy shoes and a comfortable-looking, dark brown pantsuit. It was a better choice for the drive into the mountains than the elegant dress Ginger Gage had on.

Gran poked me in the ribs. "That's Lady Jane Hampton,"

she whispered. "She's from England, but she lives in Denver now. Her husband has a business here."

Lady Jane walked to the edge of the drive and looked out at the view of the mountains and the town. Right behind her a middle-aged man hopped from the van. He grinned and gave Amy Prescott a hug around her shoulders. Then he saw Gran and me. His grin grew even broader as he bounded toward us.

"Welcome to the Silver Ridge Hotel," Gran said. She held out her right hand.

The man grabbed Gran's hand, bowed, and kissed it. "I've heard about you Colorado beauties," he said. "And I'm sure you've heard about me. I'm Mark Bannon."

Mark's latest novel was about a handsome spy who is a master at karate, speaks many languages, and travels all over the world saving beautiful women from danger. I really didn't like the book very much, so I hoped he wouldn't ask me if I'd read it. If he did, I'd have to think of something polite to say.

"Of course I've heard of you, Mr. Bannon," Gran answered. "You're famous."

"Lovely lady, don't believe everything you've heard about me," he teased. Then he added, "I'm much, much worse."

As Mark raced up the steps and into the lobby, Gran got a wicked gleam in her eyes. "He kissed my hand. He didn't kiss yours."

I pretended to frown. "Don't start trouble," I told her.

While Gran and I had been talking to Mark Bannon, the last writer had left the van. Clara Vine, a tall, elegant woman wearing sky blue pants and a pale, flowered silk blouse, was strolling toward the hotel with Uncle Jim. It hadn't taken Jim long to meet her. Somehow I wasn't surprised.

Lady Jane turned away from the scenic view with

a smile. I knew how she felt. I said to Gran, "There's something about the sweep of golden color along the mountainsides that lifts my spirits too."

"This view is nothing to brag about," said a grumpy voice next to my ear. "The trees on the East Coast are a much better show."

I turned in surprise. Facing me was a young man wearing a black turtleneck shirt and black slacks. He stared at me with a smug look on his face. I wondered if he thought we'd been in a contest—his East Coast trees against our golden aspen—and he'd won.

He gave a quick look over his shoulder and the corners of his mouth turned down. "I suppose this rustic stone building is supposed to be Rocky Mountain style," he complained. "I wish Prescott Publishing would pass on the second-rate atmosphere and put us in five-star hotels."

Before I could answer, Amy Prescott stepped up. "I heard that, Duncan," she said. "My grandfather deliberately chooses hotels with comfort and charm. He wants the writers to be inspired."

"He should see how inspired I can be surrounded by elegance," Duncan grumbled.

I was disappointed with Duncan Tyler because I enjoy reading his books. His latest was about a true crime—that horrible Texas family murder that was in the newspapers last year. After reading the book I felt I could really understand how and why it had happened. From his insight into the family members' lives, I thought Duncan would be a serious person, calm and thoughtful. Instead, he seemed small-minded and self-centered.

Duncan stomped off without another word. Amy Prescott sighed and held out her hand. "Hi," she said, "I'm Amy Prescott."

"Welcome to the Silver Ridge Hotel," Gran said. "I'm Lydia Champagne, and this is our Chief of Security, Stacy Champagne."

Amy's eyebrows rose, and she said to me, "Then you're the one I need to talk to. I have an envelope for you to keep in the hotel safe until the award dinner tonight."

"Let's put it in the safe right now," I said. I left Gran to greet Lady Jane and led Amy to my office.

I introduced Ramon to Amy. Then I said to her, "Could you take a few minutes to go over with us what happened last year? I'd like to avoid any security problems."

Amy sank into the nearest chair. "Oh. You heard about the theft," she said. "I was going to tell you about it, even though there's nothing much I can add to what you must already know. The check was in an envelope, and the envelope was in my briefcase. The briefcase was with me at all times."

I said, "From what I read, the police couldn't solve the crime."

"They asked a million questions," Amy answered. She rolled her eyes. "Almost as many questions as the writers asked."

"Do you mean that some of the writers tried to solve the theft?"

"Some of them tried. They would have asked questions in any case. Writers are like that. You'll see. They'll have plenty of questions for you while they're here."

I must have looked puzzled because she said, "Writers never take anything for granted, and they ask questions all the time. The drive up here from Denver gave me a headache. 'Could someone hiding in these woods survive during a blizzard?' 'What kind of law enforcement is there in the mountains?' 'What do you call those yellow trees?' 'Is it true that the robbers Jesse and Frank James hid out around here back in 1879?'" Amy sighed. "That should give you a general idea."

"Thanks for the warning," I said. But my mind wasn't on the writers. It was on the theft. I really needed to know how the check disappeared last year. "Amy," I said, "I've set up extra security. Deputy Sheriff Gonzales will be stationed in the office at all times until the award dinner and—"

Amy didn't let me finish. "Good," she said. "I don't want anything to happen to that check. Of course, the odds are that it won't. I've always thought that someone from the hotel we were in was responsible."

I winced. How could Amy so easily blame the hotel employees? That was so unfair that I wanted to defend them. "Are you sure the check was put in the envelope in the first place?" I snapped.

Amy didn't seem to mind my question. "Yes," she said. "I saw Huma Fenton, who is the head of our accounting department, take the check off the printer and put it into the envelope. Huma sealed the envelope. Then she handed it to me, and I put it into my briefcase. The only time it wasn't with me was when it was in the safe at the hotel."

Ramon spoke up. "You said that just before the dinner you were given the envelope from the safe? Who gave it to you?"

"The hotel's manager," Amy answered. "I was there when he opened the safe."

"From that moment on you had the envelope?"

"Yes. In my briefcase. It was next to my chair during dinner."

Ramon's next question took both Amy and me by surprise. "Who was sitting next to you?" he asked.

Amy's eyes widened. "Why, Duncan Tyler," she said. "He won the award. He expected to win because he had won the year before, and his book sales were high."

Ramon didn't give up. "Where were the others seated?"

"Let's see," Amy said. Her forehead wrinkled as she thought. "I sat at the end of the table, Ginger Gage sat at my right, and Greg sat next to her. Lady Jane was on Greg's right. Duncan was at my left. Clara sat next to Duncan, and Mark was on Clara's left."

Ramon looked as puzzled as I felt. "Wasn't there anyone who could reach the briefcase while you were eating?" he asked.

"No one," Amy said. "And I may as well tell you that the police suspected me even more than they did the writers. I'd still be under suspicion if I weren't the granddaughter of Joshua Prescott, who began our publishing company. Poor Huma has suffered too. She tells me that people sometimes look at her as though they think she pulled off the theft. And she's been with the company for twenty years." She sighed. "I wish the police had caught the thief."

"Why did your company issue a check again this year?" I asked her. "You could have given the winning author a fancy certificate and handed out the check in your office."

"I'd thought of that, and I wanted to do it," Amy agreed. "Five thousand dollars is a lot of money. But my grandfather still controls the company, and he wanted it done the way it always has been done. The check had never been stolen before, and he doesn't expect it to happen again."

"Why don't you give me the check now?" I asked.

Amy reached into her briefcase and took out a white envelope. On the upper left-hand corner were the name and address of Prescott Publishing. She handed the envelope to me.

I held it up to the light, and we could all see the shape of a check inside it. I made a small dot with a red pen in a corner of the envelope so no one could switch envelopes. Then I carefully locked it in the safe and wrote a receipt for Amy.

After she left to register at the front desk, Ramon smiled at me. "I'll never question the honesty of hotel staff. You tried not to show it, but you were steaming."

"You don't know how many times guests blame the hotel staff when something is missing," I complained. "Most of the time the guests arrive home and find what they think they lost in their own suitcases."

"Don't get mad at me for saying it, Stacy," Ramon said, "but it is possible that someone at the hotel stole the check from the safe."

I didn't get angry with Ramon. It's a deputy sheriff's job to look at all possibilities. I tried to be just as businesslike as he was. "I asked you to follow up with the Boulder police," I said. "Can you tell me if the police found fingerprints on the hotel safe? Or had it been wiped clean?"

"They found a great many prints," Ramon told me. "But they all came from the hotel staff. And there weren't any signs of a break-in."

I couldn't figure out what had happened. And the more I looked at Ramon the less businesslike I felt. "I need a hug," I said and wrapped my arms around him.

I stopped worrying, secure in the warmth of his arms around me, until Ramon spoiled it. "Stacy," he murmured against my ear, "if I were you, I wouldn't give Amy the check until she's ready to hand it to the winner."

CHAPTER 3

The writers weren't hard to keep track of during the afternoon. After lunch most of them chose to lie out by the pool or nap in their rooms. Clara Vine walked into town looking for a beauty parlor where she could get her hair done. Uncle Jim went with her to make sure, as he put it, that she wouldn't get lost.

Uncle Jim had posted a sign-up sheet in the lobby, but no one had signed up for his next morning's hike or afternoon trip to see the elk. Greg Gage and Ginger had chosen to view the stars through Jim's telescope, but theirs were the only names on the sheet. I was sure that Uncle Jim would do his best to talk Clara into signing up too. What could be more romantic than looking at the stars?

As I walked past Nadine's housekeeping office, she beckoned me to come inside. She stopped laughing long enough to say, "Shut the door."

"What's so funny?" I asked her.

"That older writer—the lady with the gray hair," Nadine said. "She asked me to tell her about the ghosts who haunt the hotel. We should get Millie Blair up here from her job at the museum. Remember that writer who was here this spring who saw Millie in her long, black 1890s dress and thought she was a ghost? Seeing Millie might be enough to stop the questions. That writer is sure we have ghosts. She says she feels the spirits."

A few minutes later I passed the front desk, and Keisha motioned to me. "Don't look now, because he's over there in the lobby," she said.

Of course I looked and saw Duncan Tyler slumped in an overstuffed chair. Either he was scowling at our carpeting or the frown was his usual expression. "What about him?" I asked.

"He said he'd read about the murder that happened here in the spring," Keisha told me in a low voice. "He asked if he could stay in the suite where the murder took place." She shivered. "He's creepy. Real creepy. I didn't want to put him there, so I told him the suite was being redecorated. Then he asked me all sorts of questions about the murder."

Lew, our head bellman, joined us. "That couple who write romantic suspense novels like to ask questions too. They wanted to know if the flowers planted around the grounds had any romantic meaning. And if we had a wedding chapel, and if we didn't, why not? And could I tell them any romantic stories about eloping couples who came here to Silver Ridge?"

I laughed. "Don't mind the questions. The writers are probably looking for plots for their next books."

The rest of the day went smoothly, and I wondered why I had worried. But just before the award dinner at seven-thirty, Amy Prescott—dressed in a terrific, black sheath dress—came to my office to pick up the check. I got a strange, nervous feeling.

Ramon raised an eyebrow as he looked at me, so I said to Amy, "Wouldn't you rather have me keep the check until it's time to present it?"

"Maybe you're right," Amy said. "Keep it until after they've eaten their desserts." She left to join the writers.

Since Prescott Publishing was a small party, we had set aside a section of our restaurant, Champagne's. We had moved some large flowerpots and planters to create a wall, separating the writers' section from the rest of the restaurant. I had gone over everything, making sure that no one could slip into the area without being seen. Then I had sat in my office next to the safe while Ramon checked the area too.

"I'd better take another look at the dining room," I said to Ramon.

"Stop worrying," he told me. "It's not time to give Amy the check."

"I hate having to wait," I said. "What am I going to do until it *is* time?"

"I've got the answer to that question," he said and kissed me.

His kiss led to another and then another. Finally I noticed the clock on my desk and jumped. "Ramon!" I said. "The writers must be almost through dinner by this time!"

I quickly brushed my hair and put on fresh lipstick. I hurried from my office toward the dining room.

As I passed the elevators, one of them opened and Clara Vine stepped out. She was wearing a red halter dress and looked terrific. I wondered if Uncle Jim had seen her in this outfit yet.

"How old are these elevators?" Clara asked me.

"We just had them inspected last month," I said. "But if you've had a problem—"

"It's not that," she said. "The hotel was built long before elevators were invented. So I just wondered when the elevators were added."

"In the Forties," I answered.

Clara thanked me and walked toward the restaurant. I remembered what Amy had said about writers asking questions and put Clara's questions out of my mind.

As I entered the restaurant, Doris, one of our waitresses, pulled me aside. "I made a switch with Henry," she said. "He's serving the writers' table."

"Why?" I asked.

She made a face of disgust. "That Mark Bannon thinks he's so great. He kissed my hand when he came in. Then he fed me a line no woman in her right mind would buy, and he asked me for a date. I'm staying far away from him."

"I'm sorry," I said. I could see that the writers had just been served our chef Eddie Jackson's famous chocolate mousse in meringues. Clara sat next to Lady Jane, but they weren't chatting, as people normally would. Lady Jane seemed pale, and I wondered for a moment if our high altitude was bothering her. Then I remembered that she lived in Denver, so she was used to high altitudes. To my surprise, Greg and Ginger sat on opposite sides of the table, ignoring each other. Amy had a fixed smile on her face, but she looked as if she would like the dinner party to be over. Mark Bannon was the only one who seemed lively, but according to Doris, he was *too* lively.

When she saw me, Amy excused herself, left the table,

and joined us. "This has been the worst dinner party ever!" she said.

"What's the trouble? If something is wrong with the food—"

Amy shook her head. "No. The food has been great. It's the writers. They're all out of sorts. These five have been nervous and jumpy all evening. And Duncan didn't even show up."

"Would you like me to go to his room and ask if he's feeling ill?"

"No, thanks," Amy said. "You don't know Duncan. He'd let everyone know loudly if he were ill. He told me earlier he had some business to take care of and would probably be a little late. I just had no idea he'd be this late."

"Are you going to present the award now or wait for him?" I asked.

Amy gave a sharp laugh. "Wait for him? If he isn't going to bother to come to the dinner, the rest of us shouldn't have to wait. Just between you and me, Duncan didn't win this year, so who cares if he's here? Let's get the check from the safe and get this over with."

I led her back to the office where Ramon was standing by the safe. I opened the safe, and the envelope was right where I'd put it. When I picked it up, I could feel the extra weight that meant the contents were still inside. And the tiny ink dot I'd made on the front proved it was the same envelope I'd put in the safe.

Amy signed for the envelope. Then she held it up to the light. We could see the shape of the check inside. "Now I'll make a little speech," she said. "I'll hand this over to the winner, and this rotten evening will be over."

Ramon and I walked back to Champagne's with her. Amy joined the writers at the table, Ramon took up a post near the exit from the restaurant, and I stood near the doors leading to the kitchen.

Amy began her speech with a couple of jokes, and the writers laughed politely. But when she held up the envelope, they leaned forward, paying close attention. She announced, "This year's award winner is—Lady Jane Hampton!"

Lady Jane smiled and stood up to receive her award, but my eyes were on the faces of the other writers. Greg and Ginger Gage applauded, but they glared at each other. Clara Vine looked as though she'd eaten something that didn't agree with her. And Mark Bannon's hearty smile wouldn't have fooled anyone. If someone had studied my own face, they probably would have seen a great sense of relief. The check had safely been given to the winner. Now I could relax.

Just as Lady Jane began to give a short speech, the kitchen door flew open and Nadine ran through. "Stacy! I need help!" she whispered in my ear. She grabbed my arm, and I could feel her trembling.

"Calm down," I said. "Tell me what happened."

Nadine took a deep breath, and spoke quietly. "I was doing the bed turn-downs and putting chocolates on the pillows like I always do," she said. "Then I opened the door to Mr. Tyler's room." She shook her head, unable to continue.

With a scared, sinking feeling I put my arm around her. "Don't try to talk," I said. "Just show me the room."

When we arrived at Room 311, Nadine used her passkey to open the door. She didn't enter the room, and she held out an arm to hold me back.

It didn't matter. I could clearly see Duncan Tyler sitting at the desk across the room. His head rested on the desk. Even from where I stood I could see that Duncan was dead.

Nadine spoke in a whisper. "There's a bloody bruise at

the front of his head. Someone hit him and hit him hard."

I looked from Duncan's body to the rest of the room. It was a mess. The top dresser drawer had been pulled out, and the mattress was half on the floor with the quilt and sheet tossed in the corner. "Was the room like this when you found him?" I asked.

She nodded, her eyes still wide and scared. "Was anyone else in the room?" I asked.

Nadine gasped. "Oh, Stacy! I never thought of that! Someone could have been in the bathroom or in the closet, and I never even looked!"

"I'll stay here in the doorway and secure the room," I told her. "You go back to the dining room and tell Ramon. Then call the police."

Nadine ran to the elevators, and I was left alone. I began wishing I wasn't Chief of Security, because I wanted to go somewhere and hide. We had put the writers in the rooms on this floor, and they were all in the restaurant so the floor was quiet. Usually there are faint sounds from television shows, or children's high-pitched voices, or someone's laughter. But this time there weren't any of the ordinary sounds of people alive and present. The floor was so silent I could hear a faint hum from the lights overhead.

As I waited for Ramon to arrive, I took another look at the room. I noticed three sheets of ordinary typing paper scattered across the floor, almost as if someone had left a trail from the table to the door. The only paper I could see on the desk was one sheet of pink stationery. It had been crumpled into a ball. On the far end of the desk was a tablet with lined yellow sheets. There wasn't anything written on it, and it looked new and unused.

There was something else I hadn't seen at first. This was a "no smoking" room, yet on the desk was an ashtray with ashes in it. It was a round metal ashtray and certainly didn't belong to the hotel. That ashtray bothered me. I could see that it was a cheap one, and I could also see that, in spite of the pile of ashes in it, there were no cigarette stubs. Had someone removed the cigarette butts? And if they had, why? Were they a brand that would be a clue to someone's identity?

There was also a tray from room service with two wineglasses on it. But there was no sign of a bottle of wine. One of the glasses had fallen over. It must have been empty because nothing had spilled onto the desk. The other glass had a red smudge at the top. I had washed enough glasses in my life to recognize the stain that lipstick leaves.

The bell on the elevator rang, and I jumped.

Ramon strode through the elevator doors the moment they opened. "You look terrible," he told me. "Are you handling this okay?"

I gulped and said, "I'm all right."

Ramon squeezed my shoulder and said, "I hate this part of the job too." As he walked into the room, I tried to follow him. But my legs shook so much I sat down with a thump on the hall carpet.

"You stay there, Stacy," Ramon said. "I'm going to examine the scene before Officer Morgan gets here and tramples all the evidence."

Ramon, with the sheriff's department, and Morgan, one of our local police officers, do not agree on how to handle a criminal investigation. Ramon wants to push for information, but Morgan likes to wait until people feel like talking. Ramon likes to follow standard police procedures, and Morgan doesn't know what standard procedures are.

I leaned against the wall, feeling sick. I thought of all the effort I had made to prevent the award from being stolen. Instead, I should have been guarding the writers. Who had done this terrible thing? And why?

CHAPTER 4

Officer Drew Morgan drove up in a few minutes, siren blaring. With the two uniformed officers he had brought, Morgan studied the scene. Then he gave an unhappy sigh. "This guy who got killed is from out of town. I'm going to have to send for all his records. The whole case is going to be difficult," he complained.

Morgan wasn't the only one who was having a difficult time. My family had followed Morgan upstairs, and they cornered me just outside the room.

"You should have called me first," Uncle Jim said. "I know your title is Chief of Security, but this is *murder*, Stacy. This is a lot for you to handle."

My father frowned. "Stacy, you called Ramon and the police, but I'm manager of the hotel. You should have notified me immediately. What were you thinking?"

"I was thinking that I should secure the scene until the police arrived," I said firmly.

"Didn't I tell you she'd have a good explanation?" Gran told Dad.

"Please don't be so angry. I thought Nadine would tell you what happened," I added.

"Well, she didn't," Dad grumbled.

"We're not angry," Gran told me. "We were just startled when Morgan came running into the hotel shouting, 'Where's the body?'"

"Don't say I'm not angry when I am," Dad said to Gran.

By this time I was getting angry too. "I did my job, Dad," I said. "I secured the room. I didn't have time to go in person to look for you."

"You wouldn't have to look for me if you kept track of the schedule. You'd know where I could be found," he said.

"I thought you wanted me to do my job the way it should be done," I answered. I tried hard to stay calm.

Uncle Jim patted my shoulder. "Stacy, you're new at this job of security. Any time you feel it's too much to handle, you can ask me for help."

I felt my face growing hot. "It's not too much to handle! I—"

"Excuse me," Ramon interrupted as he joined us. "Morgan is going to be directing this investigation, and he needs your help and the help of the hotel staff."

Before any of us could answer, Morgan walked up. He looked as cross as if he'd been part of our family argument.

"They're taking photos now," Morgan said. "Soon as the coroner gets here and does his job, they'll remove the body." He turned to Dad. "I need the hotel's phone records. Did this Duncan Tyler receive any calls or make any? Who cleaned the room last? Did any of your staff see anyone who didn't belong in the hotel on this floor? I'm going to

want to talk to everyone who has any kind of information."
He looked hopeful. "Unless somebody confesses."

Gran spoke up. "I can check with the staff. Charles,
you could go over the phone records."

Dad nodded. "You'll need some help, Mother. You can
talk to our employees at the front desk. Jim, you ask
those in housekeeping. Stacy, you—"

Morgan interrupted. "I need to talk to Stacy about that
stolen award."

Gran's hands flew to her face. "The writers' award?
The check? Don't tell me it's been stolen!"

"It's okay, Gran," I said, as Morgan took my elbow and
pulled me into the room. "I'll explain it to you later."

Ramon followed Morgan and me. "Taylor had a large
amount of cash in his pockets, so I don't think we're
looking at a crime of theft," he said.

"But someone was searching for something," I told
him. "Look at the way the room was torn up."

"Whoever searched the room was looking for
something larger than cash, because Tyler's pockets
weren't touched," Ramon insisted. Then he added, "You
may be right about a search, Stacy. I'd say the searcher
found what he—or she—was looking for in the top
dresser drawer, because the drawers below that one
weren't pulled out."

Morgan gave Ramon a sharp look. "Or Nadine
interrupted the search." Morgan turned to me. "Tell me
exactly what happened from the time Nadine came to
get you," he said.

As I did, Morgan took notes.

When I'd finished, Ramon said, "We can talk to Nadine
again. And we'd better go downstairs and talk to the

writers. We're going to have to inform them that Tyler has been murdered."

Morgan glared at Ramon as though Ramon had arranged the whole situation to annoy him. "I don't know how to talk to writers," he said. "They get paid to tell stories, so they're used to making things up. How am I supposed to know when they're lying?"

I answered for Ramon. "We can use our professional, law-enforcement instincts. Come on. Let's get this over with."

A few minutes later I led Ramon and Morgan into the dining room. I could tell immediately that the writers had already learned about the murder. Mark was glum. Greg and Ginger had changed seats and had pushed their chairs as close together as they could. Lady Jane sat upright. The stiff way she held her shoulders reminded me of my father when he's upset. Clara nervously twisted a strand of her hair. And Amy looked the way I felt—sick.

"Your grandmother and father told us about Duncan," Amy said to me.

I introduced Ramon and Officer Morgan to the writers. I wished that Morgan would stop eyeing them as though they were about to jump up and escape.

Morgan took over. After a mumbled apology for having to disturb them at such a difficult time, he said, "I don't think we need to question you separately. Just answer the questions I ask to the best of your ability." He squinted at them, adding, "And truthfully."

Clara jumped to her feet in panic. "Are you accusing us of murder?"

Ramon stepped in before Morgan could make things any worse. Ramon's voice was soothing. "No one is being accused. Officer Morgan just wants to give you the facts and learn if you can add to them. Putting the facts together may help solve this case."

Clara sat down slowly.

Morgan continued to scowl at the writers. He said, "There was no sign of forced entry. Tyler probably opened the door to the murderer. It stands to reason that the murderer might have been someone he knew."

"I don't think any of us knew him well. Duncan was a loner," Mark said.

"I always thought he was friendly," Ginger blurted out. She jumped, as though someone had poked her, then added, "Friendly for a loner, that is."

Greg didn't look at his wife. I wondered if he had signaled her to keep quiet.

"I wouldn't call Duncan a loner," Amy said. "It's just that he was such a know-it-all, he wasn't very popular." Amy shook her head and groaned. "My grandfather's going to kill me over this."

As everyone stared at Amy, startled by what she had said, she gasped. She looked from Ramon to Morgan, quickly adding, "No, no! I don't mean it. I mean that Grandfather is not going to understand how I could let one of his writers get killed."

"What could you have done to stop it?" Ramon asked quietly.

"I don't know. Maybe I should have checked when Duncan didn't come to our dinner on time." She gave another groan. "Oh, no! And Duncan hasn't turned in his manuscript yet."

"What do you mean?" Morgan asked.

Amy said, "Grandfather gave Duncan a large advance. Duncan was supposed to give him the manuscript two months ago. Only he missed his deadline. Duncan promised to deliver the completed manuscript to me this weekend."

My curiosity got the better of me. "What true crime did he write about this time?"

"This book wasn't true crime," Amy said. "It was a memoir. It was about Duncan's own life as a writer of true crime fiction."

"When you say 'manuscript' do you mean loose sheets of paper, typed or computer printed?" I asked. I could picture the scattered sheets of paper on the floor of Duncan's room.

"That's what it would look like," Amy said.

"Have you read the manuscript?" Ramon asked her. "Since it was based on Tyler's life, could it contain information that might cause problems for someone else?"

Before Amy could answer, all the writers began speaking at once. It was impossible to understand everything they were talking about. But it was easy to see that they were all hotly denying Ramon's suggestion.

Morgan raised a hand and shouted, "Quiet!"

As the noise stopped, he pointed at Lady Jane. "I heard some of what you were just saying. Would you go over it again, please?"

Lady Jane answered, "I said that perhaps Duncan wrote about his romances. It's my own experience that men can never keep their love lives secret."

Mark looked up at Morgan. "Lady Jane may be right. Duncan told me that he had something going with someone I knew. But he wouldn't say who. He just hinted that she was here this weekend. She has to be one of us."

Lady Jane looked like a child who's being naughty on purpose. "I have to admit that it wasn't me," she said.

Clara stood up again. She clutched the back of the

chair. "I hardly knew Duncan Tyler! I wasn't involved with him!"

"Then that leaves . . ." Lady Jane didn't finish her sentence, but the way she turned to look at Ginger Gage was enough.

Ginger blinked rapidly. Her mouth opened, but she didn't speak.

Greg tightly wrapped an arm around Ginger's shoulders. "Clara, you're forgetting something," he said. "I went to the same college at the same time as you and Duncan. In those days he called you his special lady."

"That was just a silly nickname," Clara cried. "We weren't romantic—not in college and not now!"

Greg raised one eyebrow. "'Special lady'? I think that was more than a nickname."

Clara stared back at Greg for a moment, then slumped down onto her chair. She spoke so softly that I could hardly hear her. "All right. We were involved, but it was for only a very short time."

"How short a time?" Ramon asked.

Clara shrugged. "I don't know."

I could tell that Ramon had those scattered typing pages in mind too. He asked Clara, "What did he tell you about the book he was writing?"

Clara looked up. "He said that it was a real tell-all book. He had some inside information about everyone."

"Who did he mean by *everyone*?"

She waved her arm to include all the writers. "Us," she said.

Mark spoke up. "I'd better confess now. You'll find out sooner or later. Duncan told me about the book too. He claimed to have written an entire chapter about me. You see, sometimes we'd go out and party. We'd get a little wild."

Lady Jane interrupted. "Are you confessing or bragging?"

Mark actually grinned. "For a guy like me, there's not much difference. I don't really mind that he had written about my adventures. But I wonder. What did Duncan know about a classy lady like you?"

Lady Jane glared at him. "Normally I do not discuss my private life," she said. "However, there is a crime to solve, so I shall tell you. Please, try not to let what I say become known outside of this room!"

Lady Jane's face went from pink to red as she said, "This is very embarrassing. I wish Duncan hadn't found out. You see, my husband was sent to take charge of the Denver branch of the family business because . . . because . . ."

I found myself leaning forward with the rest. "Because why?" I asked.

Lady Jane took a deep breath and continued. "Because I do not get along well with the Queen. For some unknown reason she does not approve of me."

Clara groaned, and Mark leaned back in his chair. "That's it?" Mark asked. "I don't think that news would be of much interest to anyone—especially to Duncan's readers."

"I seem to be the only one who's admitted anything," Clara complained.

Ginger's lower lip trembled. "I don't know if I believe you anyway," she said.

Greg took Ginger's chin and gently tilted it toward him. "Dearest, if Clara and Duncan were in love—"

"But they weren't! I know they weren't!" Ginger insisted. Tears filled her eyes.

CHAPTER 5

Again, everyone began talking at once. Finally Morgan yelled, "Quiet!" and they settled down. Morgan pointed a thick, knobby finger at Ginger and said, "Your turn, Mrs. Gage. Go ahead. Tell us what you know about this matter."

Ginger gulped and took a deep breath. She said, "I know because Clara just became engaged to some professor at the school where she teaches."

Clara gasped, but Ginger hurried on. "I met Clara while I was out shopping this afternoon. She was buying a present for her fiancé. She told me so."

"His name is Mitchell Foster," Clara said. She glared at Ginger. "I confided in Ginger in a moment of friendship and trust. I obviously shouldn't have. Mitchell and I aren't ready to announce our engagement yet."

"How did Duncan react when he found out?" Ramon asked quietly.

"I hadn't told Duncan yet," Clara mumbled. She gasped as she realized what she had said. "But it wouldn't have mattered. As I told you, it has been a long time since we were romantically involved."

"True love doesn't always run smoothly," Ginger chirped.

Clara scowled at her. "You ought to know. At the last regional booksellers convention I overheard Duncan telling you that your offstage battles with Greg would really interest your readers who think you're the perfect couple. Not to mention what might happen to the contract you have with the perfume company if the advertisers found out about your shouting matches."

Ginger let out a squeal. "Duncan promised not to tell! I mean, we had an arrangement . . . um, an agreement . . . a legal agreement, I think. That is, he told us . . ."

Greg interrupted. "We had nothing of the sort. Ginger is upset. She doesn't know what she's talking about."

"It sounds as if she's talking about blackmail," Ramon said.

Greg laughed nervously. "I'll be honest with you," he said. "Ginger and I have a terrific contract with one of the top cosmetic companies in the United States. They're soon going to launch a perfume named after our next book, *Falling Star*."

"And there will be lots of ads for the perfume on radio and in the women's magazines. Just think of all the copies of the book that will sell!" Ginger bounced in her chair like an excited child.

Morgan got right to the point. "Duncan was blackmailing you. You were afraid you'd lose your contract and maybe your readers. To my way of thinking, you thought you had a reason for getting rid of him. That's what we're looking for—motive."

Ginger gasped, but Greg's voice rose. "We're not the only ones here with a motive for murder."

"Would you like to explain that statement?" Ramon asked.

Greg's glance shifted to each of the writers around him, and his brave attitude disappeared. "You're the detectives," he said. "It's your job to figure it out."

The questioning went on and on. After a while, I realized that no one had said anything new. I looked at my watch, surprised to find that it was nearly two in the morning. I wondered if the others felt as exhausted as I did.

Finally Ramon turned to Morgan. "Have you any more questions?"

Morgan just shook his head, so Ramon said to the writers, "Then I think we're finished—for tonight, at least. I've been told that you're booked for the entire weekend. Please don't leave the Silver Ridge city limits. We may need to question you tomorrow."

The writers quickly left the room. I took a tray with their water glasses to the kitchen, then caught up with Lady Jane near the elevators.

"Would you like me to put your award check in the hotel safe?" I asked.

"That's a good idea," she said. She pulled the envelope out of her handbag and offered it to me, but I didn't take it.

"Come to my office," I said. "You'll have a deposit form to sign, and I'll have to give you a receipt." I wanted to follow every rule so that we could avoid any further trouble.

I stopped in surprise when I pushed open the door of the office. Nadine was curled up on the short sofa with her coat draped over her legs. She was sound asleep, even though the light was on. Gran sat at my computer, and Morgan leaned over her shoulder, his eyes on the screen.

"We can easily bring up the charges to Mr. Tyler's room," Gran said.

"Excuse me," I said softly. I didn't want to wake Nadine. "I'm going to put the award check in the safe for Lady Hampton."

Lady Jane and I filled out the proper forms, and I unlocked the safe.

"I see you have one of those old-fashioned, combination safes," she said. "Why aren't you using a new, high-tech one?"

Morgan whirled to stare at her. "How do you know so much about safes?" he asked.

"I had to learn enough about safes to write about them," Lady Jane answered. "In my next-to-the-last mystery novel I had one of the characters steal an important government document from a safe."

"So you know how a criminal opens a safe?" I asked.

Lady Jane laughed. "If you're suspecting that I opened the safe in Boulder last year, you're dead wrong. I didn't open that safe, and I doubt if I could open *any* safe. My character had the proper tools that could bypass the burglar alarm and open the safe." She counted on her fingers. "One, I don't have the tools. And, two, I'm terribly clumsy with any kind of machinery. I've set off my own burglar alarm at home more than once. You have nothing to fear from me."

Morgan shrugged, and I felt uneasy. I hadn't thought about all the research mystery writers need to do in order to write about crime. There was no telling what these writers knew.

I made sure the check was in the envelope, then put it into the safe. I stood in front of the door as I spun the dial so Lady Jane wouldn't know what numbers were used.

"Thank you," Lady Jane said. "And good night."

As she left the office Gran pointed at the computer screen. "Here's the record from Duncan Tyler's room. No phone calls came in for him, and just one was made from his room. The only other charge is for room service."

"What was Tyler's exact room service order?" Morgan asked.

Gran pushed a few more keys. "A bottle of white wine and the small snack tray."

"How many people would that serve?"

"That depends. He might have wanted it for himself. However, there's enough food to serve four people if they aren't too hungry."

"How many glasses did Tyler ask for?"

"It doesn't say," Gran told him. "He'd be given two wineglasses unless he asked for more."

There was a knock at the door, and Ramon came into the office. "I've got the information about the schedule," he said.

"Are you ready to ask me questions?" Nadine asked in a sleepy voice. She sat up and stretched. Between yawns, she said, "Stacy, don't ever try to sleep on this couch. It's really uncomfortable."

Morgan came around the desk. "Do you want some coffee, Nadine?"

She made a face. "I want to brush my teeth and sleep in my own bed. I thought you wanted to ask me about the murder."

Morgan nodded. "Okay. Who was the last person to clean Tyler's room?"

"Angela," Nadine said. "Also, I made sure the rooms on the third floor were ready before the guests arrived."

"Who checked Tyler into the hotel?" Morgan asked.

"Dad did," I answered.

"Who took his luggage upstairs?"

"Lew Parker," I said. "But Lew went home before any of this happened. He'll be coming in just before nine A.M."

Ramon had a question. "Who brought the wine to Tyler's room?"

"The person who took the wine upstairs would have put his or her initials on the order to show it was delivered," Gran said. "The order sheet would be in the kitchen. We don't bother to put things like that into the computer."

"I'll check the room service orders," I offered. As Morgan and Ramon began to ask Nadine to tell them about finding Tyler's body, I headed toward the kitchen.

Dad met me in the lobby. "I've been wondering about something," he said. "It's not very important, but maybe I should tell Drew Morgan."

"What is it?" I asked.

"Amy Prescott from Prescott Publishing made the reservations for this weekend. The next day a man named Mitchell Foster telephoned and said he was Clara Vine's fiancé. He asked for a room for this weekend. Then, two days ago, Clara Vine telephoned and canceled his reservation."

"What's bothering you about that?" I asked.

Dad shrugged. "I thought at the time that she sounded terribly upset. Her voice was stuffy, as if she'd been crying."

"Maybe their engagement had been broken," I said.

Dad looked embarrassed. "I try not to involve myself with the personal lives of our guests. But because of the murder . . . well, any bit of information might be important."

"I agree," I told him. "Tell Morgan."

As I walked to the file cabinet in the kitchen offices,

my footsteps echoed. I looked through the pages of orders until I found the right sheet. At five-thirty, Duncan Tyler had ordered a bottle of the house white wine and a small snack tray. Fifteen minutes later, Alicia had brought it to his room. I flipped through the rest of the evening's orders. There had been only one other delivery to the authors. Lady Jane had ordered champagne just before seven. Champagne for one? Or two? I wondered.

On my way back to the office with the information, I ran into Uncle Jim.

"Stacy," he said, "do they know yet what time the poor guy was murdered?"

"Not until they get the coroner's report," I said. "Why?"

"I guess it's not important," Uncle Jim said. "There's just something on my mind. I was wondering if I should tell Ramon what I know."

"What do you know? Why don't you tell me?" I asked.

"Okay," Uncle Jim said. "I keep forgetting that you are the hotel's Chief of Security. Just before the dinner, Greg Gage asked me what time it was. Then he looked at his watch and told me it was seven-thirty. He said it again. Now that I think of it, he seemed to be making a special point of telling me what time it was."

I waited for him to make his point. When he didn't say anything else, I asked, "What time was it really?"

"Don't ask me," Uncle Jim said. "You know I don't like wearing a watch." He sighed. "Do you see what I mean? That's why I don't know whether or not to tell Ramon. Maybe it really was seven-thirty."

CHAPTER 6

The next morning I awoke to see Gran putting one of the room service trays on the table by my bed. On the tray were a pot of tea and one of the large cinnamon rolls from the coffee shop downstairs. The fragrance of the hot, buttery roll was too tempting to resist, so I sat up and broke off a bite. I popped it into my mouth.

"Jim says we'll have sunny weather today," Gran told me. She smiled cheerfully, but there were dark circles under her eyes.

"Why are you bringing me breakfast?" I asked. Then I glanced at the clock and gasped. "It's nine o'clock already! Who turned off my alarm?"

"You were up so late last night, I thought you needed the rest," Gran said. She closed my window and sat on the end of my bed. "I want to talk to you, Stacy. Why didn't you tell me about the award being stolen last year? Do you think I'm too old to help?"

I was surprised to hear the hurt in her voice. I tried to ease the situation. "Of course not," I said. "Hotel security is my job. I just did my best to protect the check."

Gran sighed. "I wish you'd count me as part of your team."

There was Dad's word—*team*—again. "I just wanted to spare you the worry," I said. "You're doing so much already."

Gran patted my hand and said, "You can still rely on me, Stacy dear." I knew she felt better when she abruptly changed the subject. "By the way, Tess O'Connor wants you to drop by the store. She said she has something she wants to ask you."

I groaned. Tess is pushy. When Tess wants to talk to me, she wants to sell me something. "Did she say anything about a tent?" I asked. "I've spent the last six weeks trying to convince Tess that I don't need or want a tent."

"Tess said to tell you she sold the tent to one of the tourists," Gran said. "She wants to see you about something else. I think you should talk to her."

I was sure that Tess had another white elephant she wanted me to buy. However, an hour later I did start out to visit Tess. But as I walked down the hotel's drive, I spotted Ramon at the end of the drive. There went my good intentions. I'd rather spend my time with Ramon than with Tess.

As I reached him, Ramon pulled me close and gave me a kiss. "Anybody confess yet?" he said and grinned.

"None of the writers have come downstairs. For all I know they're still asleep."

"Not a guilty conscience in the lot? That's going to make it tough for us investigators," Ramon teased.

"Walk with me a little ways," I said. "I do have some information, for what it's worth. Did Uncle Jim tell you about his conversation with Greg Gage yesterday evening?"

"Yes," Ramon said.

As we headed into town I felt the nip of the clear fall air. A few aspen leaves scattered the walkway like spilled drops of gold. "Why do you think Greg pointed out that it was seven-thirty over and over again?" I asked Ramon.

Ramon shrugged. "I have no idea. According to Jim, Greg told him he was waiting for his wife to finish changing into her dinner dress. There was probably nothing to the conversation, but I'll have a talk with Greg."

"Could it have something to do with the time of the murder?" I asked. "Do you know yet what time that was?"

"Not yet," Ramon said. "We should be getting a report from the coroner this morning."

"There's something else that's been puzzling me," I told him. "Do you know where that cheap metal ashtray in Duncan's room came from? It's not ours. In fact, that's a non-smoking room."

"Mark told me he brought the ashtray with him. Mark smokes cigars."

"He must have smoked an awful lot of cigars while he was in Duncan's room. Did you notice the pile of ashes in that ashtray?"

"I haven't received a report from the lab yet, but I'd guess that wasn't all cigar ash. I think someone burned some paper in that ashtray," Ramon said.

An idea flashed into my mind. "Could someone have burned some of Duncan's manuscript?"

"Maybe only a page or two, nothing more than that." Ramon stopped and looked back, his gaze moving up to the third-floor windows in the hotel. "If someone was burning paper in the room, why didn't the smoke alarm go off?"

That was a question I could answer. "The desk is next

to the window. If the smoke went out the open window, it wouldn't set off the alarm."

Ramon was still puzzled. "If someone burned one page of the manuscript, what happened to the rest of it?"

"What about the typewritten pages lying on the floor?" I asked. "Weren't they part of the manuscript?"

"They could be," Ramon said. "There were only three sheets, numbered three, four, and five. What was written on them was all about Duncan himself. None of them mentioned other writers."

"How many pages were in the manuscript? Do you know?"

"Amy could only guess," Ramon said. "She told me it could be anywhere from two hundred fifty pages to four hundred."

"A package that thick would be hard to hide," I said.

Ramon took my hand and we began walking again. "Someone has hidden it, but we haven't found it," he said. "Morgan woke up a judge, got warrants, and searched the writers' rooms last night. We didn't find any sign of the manuscript."

"There was a pink sheet of paper on Duncan's desk," I said. "What was that?"

"It was a love letter, I think," Ramon said.

I pulled my hand away from his. "What do you mean, you think? I'm not going to send you anything in writing if you can't tell a love letter when you see one."

Ramon grinned. "Hear me out. I'll tell you what it said. 'Duncan, I am counting every minute until we are together.' Even though the paper was perfumed, the message was typed and not signed. Would you type a love letter?"

I moved a little closer, and for a moment I rested my

head on his shoulder. "Are you asking as A—a deputy on a case? Or B—as someone who would like me to write him a love letter?"

"Business first," Ramon said. "We'll get to plan B later. Do you have any ideas about why it wasn't signed?"

"Sure," I said. "Duncan would know who sent it with or without a signature. Also, I'm sure he'd recognize the perfume. Some women are well known for their special perfume."

Ramon leaned down and sniffed behind my ear. "Umm . . . soap," he said.

"Be serious," I told him. "Do you suppose the note was from Clara?"

"Clara's fiancé had planned to come to Silver Ridge. She wouldn't be likely to send Duncan a note."

"If Clara and Mitchell Foster had broken their engagement, she might." I told Ramon about Clara canceling Mitchell's reservation and Dad's guess that she'd been crying. "Maybe we could match the lipstick found on the wineglass with one of the authors," I added.

"The glass is at the lab," Ramon told me. "There were actually three glasses used for wine. There was the glass with lipstick and the wineglass that had been knocked over on the tray, and I found another glass on the floor."

"But Alicia brought only two wineglasses up to the room," I said.

"The third glass was a drinking glass, but there was some wine in the bottom."

"That means three people were in the room."

"I'm going to look over the room again this morning," Ramon said. "I may have a better idea what happened after that."

"I've got to see Tess," I told him, so we kissed good-bye. Kissing "hello" was much nicer.

When I arrived at O'Connor's store, I stopped and took a deep breath. The store smelled like Christmas.

"It's the eggnog coffee I'm brewing," Tess said. "I thought if I remind the customers that they can do their Christmas shopping early, I might increase sales."

"But it's only September," I said.

Tess ignored my comment. She leaned close and in a low voice said, "I heard about that murder."

"I'm sure everyone has heard by this time," I said.

A customer wandered into the store and Tess called to her, "Take a look at the stack of paperback books by the window. They've all been autographed by the authors. They'd make great gifts."

I glanced over at the books. "They're by the authors up at the hotel," I said in surprise. "When did they autograph for you?"

Tess looked smug. "Authors love to autograph their books," she said. "All I had to do was ask. They each came by yesterday afternoon." She lowered her voice again. "That's what I wanted to talk to you about. Do you think I should tell the police?"

"I don't know," I said. "Did anything strange take place while they were here?"

Tess didn't hear me. The woman who'd been looking at the books was walking back toward the door. Tess ran up to her. "I can't let you leave empty-handed," she said. "How about buying an umbrella? We're having a special on our pink umbrellas, and I heard on the radio that we're in for a wet afternoon."

The woman thought a moment. Then she decided to buy a pink umbrella.

I waited until she left and said to Tess, "I thought it was supposed to be sunny today."

Tess wasn't embarrassed. "Maybe it was the weather for Denver that I heard. It doesn't matter. As I was telling you, during the afternoon the writers wandered in and signed the books they wrote. I can't charge more for signed copies, but they should sell faster."

"Did the writers come over here together?"

"No, that poor man, Duncan Tyler, came first. He asked me a lot of questions about how many of his books I had ordered. I had quite a few on hand. His last book hasn't sold very well."

I wondered what Tess wanted to tell the police. "Did one of the other writers come in and argue with him?" I asked.

"No. Duncan Tyler bought a box of fudge and left."

"Then what did you want to tell the police?"

"Wait, I'm getting to it," Tess said. "Next Lady Jane Hampton came over. She's not what I expected her to be like. She asked me if her books are popular here in Silver Ridge, and she bought a sweatshirt. Then Clara Vine came in. It was after my dinner break, so it must have been six-thirty or later. She took a long time. She looked at everything in the store, but she finally decided on a music box with a mountain scene painted on it. She had it gift wrapped for her fiancé."

"So far you haven't told me anything unusual," I said.

Tess went on as though I hadn't spoken. "Ginger Gage came in while Clara was here, and they started talking. Clara had a lot to tell Ginger about how much in love she is and how she just got engaged." Tess looked at me from the corners of her eyes. "You understand that I'm not a snoop, don't you? I couldn't help but overhear."

"Of course," I said.

"Let me tell you, Ginger really knows her business," Tess said. "She asked me all sorts of questions about how I order, and what my sales are, and what percentage of books are returned."

"Did she tell you about the perfume contract and the new book, *Falling Star?*"

"Oh, yes. They're going on sale in time for Valentine's Day next February. Just in time for Ginger too, if you ask me." Tess winked and added, "Her clothes are good quality, but they're well worn. I used to think all writers were rich, but I was wrong. Clara told me that writers don't get insurance or pension plans or benefits. That's why she teaches writing. She doesn't make enough as a writer to support herself."

"Do you really think Ginger needs money?"

"Yes, I do. I got to thinking. Lady Jane's husband runs a business in Denver, and Clara teaches, but the other writers don't have second jobs. Officer Morgan ought to give that some thought."

"Tell him," I said. I made my excuses, firmly resisting one of the marked-down, pink umbrellas, and left the shop. Tess had given me something to think about.

CHAPTER 7

Mark met me on the porch as I came back to the hotel. The morning air was brisk, and he wore a jacket buttoned up to the neck. "Is there an airport near here?" he asked.

"No," I said. "Silver Ridge is a small town. We've never had air service."

"But what about someone with his own plane? Is there a long, flat road where a small plane could land? Maybe secretly?"

Mark's questions made me curious. Why did he want to know where to secretly land a plane in Silver Ridge? The only answers I came up with were drug smuggling, political prisoners escaping, or a secret meeting between government spies.

He broke into my thoughts. "I guess I'll have to make it a hot air balloon."

I was startled. "What are you talking about?"

Mark laughed. "My book, the one I'm working on now. I was hoping my main character could rescue the victim and fly off in his plane. But since there's nowhere for a plane to land around here, maybe a hot air balloon would be better."

I left Mark working on the plot for his book. As I walked into the lobby, Lew hurried toward the elevators with a Denver paper. He stopped when he saw me.

"I heard what happened last night," Lew said. "Do they know what time Mr. Tyler was killed?"

"Not yet," I answered.

Lew stepped close to me and spoke quietly. "Last night I saw someone coming out of Duncan Tyler's room. I was bringing champagne to Lady Jane, so it must have been around seven."

"Who was he?" I asked quickly.

"I don't know. And it might have been a 'she,' not a 'he.' I just had a quick look at the person's back. Then Lady Hampton opened the door. Whoever it was was wearing a dark coat, slacks, and a hat." He thought a moment and added, "I do remember that the person was carrying a package."

The manuscript? Excitedly, I held my hands apart. "Was the package about this big?" I asked.

Lew shrugged. "Maybe. That looks about right."

"Lew, you'd better talk to Ramon," I said. "He should be in the office."

"Soon as I take this paper to Miss Prescott," Lew said. He headed into one of the elevators.

I checked my office. Ramon was sitting on the uncomfortable sofa. He had an assortment of papers spread out around him. I told him what Lew had told me.

There was a knock on the office door, but it wasn't Lew.

It was Morgan. He took a pink umbrella from under his arm and placed it on my desk. "I've been over at O'Connor's store," he told Ramon. "Tess thought she had some information to give me. It didn't amount to anything."

Ramon moved some of the papers from the sofa so Morgan could sit down. I perched in my desk chair and listened as Ramon said, "I've been going over the medical examiner's report. As we thought, death was the result of a strong blow to the head."

Morgan nodded. "Tyler was sitting at his desk when someone hit him with that bottle of wine."

"It looks like that's what happened," Ramon said.

"Duncan left us a schedule," Morgan told me.

Ramon stretched to hand me one of the pages of his report. It was a photocopy of a typed sheet of paper showing a list of names and times. "We think that Tyler met with the other writers at the times noted on that list," Ramon said.

"They all had appointments with him?" I read the page. "Mark Bannon at five, Clara Vine at five-thirty, Greg and Ginger Gage at six, and Lady Jane at six-thirty. Lady Jane must have returned to her room before seven, because Lew told me he delivered a bottle of champagne to her around seven."

Ramon said. "According to Lady Jane, she only talked to Tyler a few minutes. When he demanded money from her, she refused and left."

"Duncan must have been trying to blackmail every one of the writers," I said.

Morgan nodded. "His scheme must have worked. He had a lot of cash on him."

"What did the coroner give as the estimated time of death?" I asked.

"Seven, give or take half an hour either way," Morgan said.

"Seven is when Lew saw someone leave Duncan's room."
I told Ramon and Morgan what Lew had told me.

"We'd better talk to him," Morgan said.

"Stacy met Lew a few minutes ago," Ramon explained.
"He told her he'd talk to us as soon as he finished a delivery."

I jumped up and said, "I'll see if I can find him."

Lew wasn't in the lobby, and he wasn't in the kitchen.
He hadn't turned in his delivery slip to room service yet,
so I took the elevator upstairs. Lew wasn't in the hall, so
I knocked on the door of Amy's room.

"Coming," Amy called, but there was a long wait until she
answered the door. Her eyes were red, and I could tell she'd
been crying. Behind her I saw the Denver newspaper spread
out on the foot of the bed. "I'm looking for Lew," I told Amy.

"Lew?" Amy asked.

"He brought you the newspaper."

"Oh," she said. "He left a long time ago."

I started to turn away, but Amy looked so miserable I
asked, "Are you all right?"

"Yes," Amy said. "No. Oh, you work in a family business.
You know how difficult things can be." She stepped aside.
"Please come in, Stacy. I need to talk to you."

Amy closed the door and sat on the end of the bed, so
I took the chair next to the desk. She pulled a tissue out
of the pocket of her slacks and wiped her eyes.

"I've been talking to my grandfather on the phone.
He's really upset about what happened to Duncan Tyler."
She looked desperate. "It wasn't my fault."

"Surely, your grandfather wouldn't blame *you*," I said.

"He thinks I should have done something, but how could
I know Duncan was going to be murdered?" Amy twisted her
fingers together. "Grandfather ordered me to keep an eye on

the writers so there wouldn't be any more trouble. But he also insisted that I stay in my room with the door locked, just to be safe. What am I supposed to do?"

"Don't be upset about the mixed messages," I told her. "He's just worried about you."

She sighed. "I guess he is. And he's probably trying to figure out why the writers are upset about what Duncan wrote about them. They can't really believe my grandfather would print a book that would hurt their reputations."

"Do you have any idea what Duncan wrote in that missing manuscript?" I asked.

Amy shook her head. "I only know what Grandfather told me. The book was supposed to contain stories and anecdotes about Duncan's writing life."

"Some of his experiences as a writer might have involved other writers," I said. "Is there any chance that Duncan might have been blackmailing your grandfather?"

Amy sat upright, startled. "Grandfather?" She laughed. "My grandfather has led a very dull life, by some people's standards. He married my grandmother after high school, and they've worked hard all their lives."

My father would never approve of being rude to a guest, but there was another question I had to ask. "What about you? Was Duncan blackmailing you?"

"I've had the dullest life of all," Amy answered. "I studied hard in high school and worked part-time for grandfather. I couldn't even join the marching band like I wanted to, because that took too much time away from study and work."

"You've been out of high school for at least fifteen years," I reminded Amy.

"I know," she said. "But college life was the same mix of hard work and study. I gave up trying to do something on my own. I just kept trying to please my family."

Amy's life and mine had taken very different turns. When I finished college, I wanted to stay and work at the hotel, but my father sent me away. No one in my family had asked me to stay. I saw a different side of things when I learned that my father was trying to keep me from feeling trapped by the family business. On the other hand, Amy's family had wanted to include her in the family business right from the start, and she *did* feel trapped.

"Have you talked to your family about how you feel?" I asked her.

"I'm the only grandchild. I've been told over and over that I have to keep the business going." She tilted her head and studied me. "Hasn't it been the same for you?"

"I spent some time doing other things," I told her. "This is my first year back at the hotel. I came back because I wanted to."

Amy looked close to tears again. "But what if you never wanted to come back?"

I thought a moment. "If you weren't working for your grandfather, what would you be doing?"

"I don't know," she said softly.

Our talk had calmed her, so I left and went back downstairs. As I passed Gran's office, I heard a deep voice raised in anger, so I pushed open the door. I nearly bumped into a middle-aged man who was wearing an expensive black coat and a black racing cap. He turned around and glared at me before he spoke again to Gran.

"I want answers now," he demanded. He was nearly shouting.

Gran tried hard to be polite. "Why don't you let me introduce you to our Chief of Security. Stacy, this is Mr. Walter Hampton. He's Lady Jane's son."

Mr. Hampton turned his anger on me. "Where can I find

the person in charge of this murder case?" he growled.

Behind me I heard Morgan's voice. He spoke in the deadly serious tone he uses when he's handing out speeding tickets. "I'm Officer Morgan with the Silver Ridge Police Department," he said. "Who are you?"

"I'm Walter Hampton. I'm Lady Jane Hampton's son."

Ramon stepped into the room and stood with his shoulder touching mine. Calmly, Ramon said, "Mr. Hampton, your mother and the other writers have been helping us by giving us information about the victim."

I glanced up at Ramon. He was watching Mr. Hampton intently.

Mr. Hampton looked back and forth from Ramon to Morgan. He took a long breath and spoke in a normal voice. "I want to get my mother out of this crime-ridden place and take her back to Denver."

Gran protested. "Silver Ridge is not crime-ridden, and the hotel is safe. This area has had a very low burglary rate, no armed robberies, and only an occasional murder."

Mr. Hampton's mouth opened, but before he could say a word Ramon spoke firmly. "I'm sure you and your mother want to help us solve this case. We need your mother to be on hand to answer questions."

"My mother doesn't know anything about this crime or any other crime," Mr. Hampton insisted.

Morgan and I looked at each other. We were remembering all that Lady Jane had said the night before about opening a safe.

Gran added, "I'm sure you don't need to worry about your mother, because—"

She didn't finish the sentence. We heard a loud scream coming from the direction of the lobby.

CHAPTER
8

Ramon was quick. He was out of the office before the scream faded. Morgan raced after him. I was right behind. We ran across the lobby to the hallway where Greg stood, holding open the door to the ballroom. Greg had an odd, embarrassed look on his face. Clara leaned against him, clinging to his shoulder, and she looked pale. I hoped she wasn't going to faint.

We all squeezed past Greg and Clara as we ran into the ballroom. By the time I caught up to Ramon, he was kneeling beside a body lying face down on the polished floor. For a moment I wanted to scream too. It was Lew.

"He's breathing," Ramon reported. "He's got a strong pulse."

Behind me Morgan spoke into his portable phone. I heard him ask for an ambulance. Shaking with a wave of fury at whoever had hurt Lew, I knelt next to Ramon.

In a very short time the paramedics ran into the room with their emergency equipment and stretcher. I stood up, moving out of the way. But I tripped over something and nearly lost my balance. One of the heavy ceramic vases that decorate the ballroom lay broken on the floor. I looked at the table where the vase should be standing. The fabric flowers from the vase had been tossed across the top of the table. Someone must have grabbed the vase and hit Lew with it.

As the police photographer's camera flashed, I wondered who had lured Lew into the ballroom and hit him. And why? Was what Lew saw the night before that important?

Ramon put a hand on my shoulder as the paramedics carried Lew out to the ambulance. "His vital signs are strong. I think he'll make it, Stacy," he said.

Then he turned away to talk to the police photographer. I walked out to the lobby to reassure any of the guests who had heard the siren and had come downstairs to find out what had happened. I looked for Lady Jane and her son, who must be even more upset by this time. But I didn't see them. Ginger Gage had showed up and was clinging to her husband.

Morgan strode up to me. "Where's a quiet place where I can talk to these people?"

"How about the meeting room across the hall?" I suggested. I led the way, opened the room, and set up a few folding chairs.

Clara dropped into the first chair she reached. Ginger clung tightly to Greg's arm, even though it made it hard for him to hold her chair for her. I expected Morgan to take charge, but he hadn't come into the room.

As I poked my head outside the door, I found Morgan and Ramon disagreeing with each other's procedures again.

"You should question suspects one at a time," Ramon insisted.

"They were together after the banquet and look how

much they told us," Morgan said.

Ramon's voice was firm. "I let you talk me into that once, but I want to handle this session the right way."

Morgan shrugged. "We've got three of them in the meeting room ready to talk. We'd better get in there before we miss something important."

Ramon and Morgan hadn't missed a thing. The suspects weren't speaking to each other. Morgan and Ramon pulled out chairs and sat with the writers, but I stood leaning against the back wall. I didn't want to sit with the person who had hit Lew.

I was having trouble dealing with my feelings. I wanted to be a good Chief of Security and handle things calmly and clearly. But at the same time I wanted to forget my job and shout at these people until the one who had hit Lew confessed.

Morgan was the first to speak. He glared at Greg and Clara. "I'd like to know what the two of you were doing in an empty ballroom."

"We wanted to talk privately," Greg said. "We tried a few doors, but they were locked. The only open door we found was the one that led into the ballroom."

Morgan asked, "What kind of talk did you need a private room for?" The way he said the word *talk* made it sound as if Greg and Clara would be doing everything *except* talking.

Ginger jumped to her feet. "I want to know the answer to that too!"

Greg pulled her back into her chair. "Darling, it's not what you think."

Ginger faced him. "Ever since the award dinner, you and Clara have been sharing some secret."

"How can you think that?" Greg said.

"You've never kept a secret from me before," Ginger complained. "I don't like being treated this way."

Clara perched on the edge of her chair, the way she had the night of the award dinner. I wondered if she was going to try to run away. "Why don't you trust your husband?" she asked Ginger.

Ginger leaped to her feet again. "Why can't you stay away from my husband?"

"It's your own fault!" Clara jumped up, and her chair fell over. "Your husband begged me to say that Duncan was *my* boyfriend to cover up the fact that you were having an affair with Duncan."

Ginger gasped and sat down, looking stunned.

Clara hadn't finished. "I don't know why your husband bothered. Everyone knew about you and Duncan."

I glanced at Greg. He sat with his head in his hands, so I couldn't see his face. I began to look at the evidence in a new way. The pink note must have been from Ginger. She hadn't signed it, so if it somehow got into her husband's hands, he wouldn't know she had written it. I studied Ginger. I still couldn't understand why any woman would be interested in Duncan.

Ginger struggled to her feet and faced Clara. "I want to know what the secret is between you and my husband."

Clara folded her arms over her chest. "I don't have to tell you."

Greg stood up and took his wife's hand. "Dearest, there was nothing romantic between Clara and me. Like Mark said, I knew Duncan in college, and I knew he used to call Clara his special lady because—"

"Don't say anything else!" Clara interrupted. But Greg didn't listen to her.

"Because she wrote his term papers for him," he said.

"Then she must have loved him," Ginger said softly.

"No, she had a regular business writing term papers. She charged by the page."

Clara stepped toward them. She shook with anger, and when she spoke she said each word carefully, as if it were hard for her to talk. "You're as rotten as Duncan. You know if the information gets out, I'll lose my reputation and my teaching job." She gave a little sob. "If you're going to tell my secret, then I have to tell yours."

Morgan nodded at Ramon, as if to say, "I told you so."

The writers were giving out lots of information, but the wrong kind. I wanted to find out why Lew had been attacked. I wanted the writers to start talking about that.

"Wait a minute!" Greg cried. "It was all just a boyish prank. It didn't mean anything."

Clara turned to Ramon. "When we were in college, Greg stole a check from his father's checkbook and forged his dad's name."

"Look," Greg said, "I'd run up a good-sized tab at the local restaurant. The owner threatened to go to my father, so I wrote the guy a check. Everyone was happy. Okay?"

"I don't think your father knew about the check," Clara said. "You told me once that his secretary took care of his accounts, so he probably didn't even know what you'd done. If he was so happy that your bill was paid, then why didn't he sign the check himself? Why did you have to forge his name?"

"That was to make it easier for him," Greg said. He looked around the room at us, but he could see that none of us believed him. "That was years ago," Greg said. "It's the only time I've ever done it."

"We can give your father a phone call and confirm

that," Ramon said.

"No! Don't do that!" Greg cried. "Look, maybe he didn't know about the check. Maybe he would have given me the check if he'd thought of it."

Ginger looked at Greg with disgust. "You stole the check and signed it!"

"It was Duncan's idea," Greg said. "He told me my dad wouldn't know the difference, and if I didn't pay the tab I'd go to jail."

Just then the meeting room door opened. Walter Hampton marched into the room with Lady Jane trailing behind him. "After what happened this afternoon, I demand that my mother be allowed to go back to Denver at once!" Hampton cried.

Lady Jane glanced at Ginger's tearstained face, Clara's red eyes, and Greg's sheepish look. "I do believe we may be interrupting something. Have we come at a bad time?" she asked.

Hampton shook his head. "That doesn't matter. It should only take a minute for the police to agree that you can leave."

"I thought you understood that your mother is a witness. We need her here in Silver Ridge to answer questions," Ramon said. I could tell he was prepared for an argument. But before Hampton could answer back, Mark Bannon wandered into the room.

"Oh, here's where you all are," Mark said. "Did you know that the nature hike has been canceled?"

"I thought we canceled all the events out of respect for Duncan," Lady Jane said.

"We were asked to meet here so we could talk about the poor man who was hurt," Clara informed Mark.

"Who was hurt? What happened?" Mark asked.

"Didn't you see or hear the ambulance?" Ginger cried.

Mark looked puzzled. "No. I just came downstairs."

Morgan explained to him that a bellman had been knocked unconscious and had been taken to the clinic. "We believe that Lew may have seen someone leaving Tyler's room last night around seven," he said.

"Someone wearing a dark coat, slacks, and a hat," I added.

Lady Jane's voice trembled. "Is the person the bellman saw the one who murdered Duncan?"

"It could be," Ramon answered.

"But we were all here for the award dinner at seven-thirty," Ginger said quickly. "It couldn't have been any of us."

"I understand you arrived a little *after* seven-thirty," Ramon said.

Ginger gulped and quickly glanced at Greg.

Mark spoke up. "I can prove I didn't murder Duncan," he said. "During the time you're talking about, I walked down to the drugstore in town and bought a cigar. Look, I still have the cigar with me. Somehow, it didn't seem right to smoke it last night." He fished in his shirt pocket and brought out a wrapped cigar that he waved in front of us.

Greg and Ginger glanced at each other. "Ginger and I were together the entire evening," Greg said firmly.

"No, you weren't," Clara said. "Ginger was by herself when I went to O'Connor's shop around six. We stayed there talking until close to six-thirty."

Ginger smiled. "That gives Clara and me an alibi."

"No, it doesn't," Morgan said. "That time frame is too early to work as an alibi."

Ginger shrugged. "Then that means I'm back to being your alibi, Greg."

Lady Jane shook her head. "Ginger, you were alone when I saw you outside Duncan's room just before seven o'clock."

Ginger paused a minute. With wide eyes she looked at Ramon and then at Morgan. "Oh, oh. There's something I should have told someone. When I dropped by Duncan's room last night, Lady Jane was leaving."

"Was Duncan alive at that time?" Ramon asked.

Mr. Hampton spoke up. "My mother doesn't want to answer any more questions until she has talked to a lawyer."

"Don't be silly," Lady Jane told him. "Everyone knows that Duncan was alive when I left his room."

Ginger spoke sharply. "What went on while you were in Duncan's room?"

"Nothing much," Lady Jane said. "Duncan wrote me a letter asking me to meet him at six-thirty Friday to talk over something important. When we met, he told me if I paid him enough, he'd take the chapter about me out of his book."

Mark nodded. "That sounds familiar. Duncan wrote to tell me to meet him at five. Then he offered to drop something highly personal about me from the book. The only catch was that I had to come up with a great deal of money."

Clara looked up. "We all got the same kind of letter from Duncan. I phoned the others to find out. He asked me to meet him at five-thirty. And, of course, he asked for money—twenty-five thousand dollars. I had to close my savings account and take something from my retirement fund." Her voice dropped as she said, "And I paid him."

Morgan's stare drilled into the eyes of each of the writers. "Anybody else pay Tyler?"

No one answered, so Morgan turned to Ginger. "You never told us what you were doing at Tyler's door at seven o'clock. That wasn't the time of your appointment."

"Yes, it was," Ginger said. "That is, we were supposed to come at six, but I couldn't make it, so we came at seven. Only we really didn't come at seven. I think we got to Duncan's room around six-forty. It doesn't matter. Duncan was alone. Greg and I told Duncan we didn't have the kind of money he wanted us to pay, and we left. But after Greg had gone downstairs, I thought if I asked Duncan nicely, maybe he would drop the chapter about Greg and me for the sake of our friendship, so I went back. It must have been close to seven o'clock . . . I think."

"What did Duncan tell you when you came the second time?" Ramon asked.

"He wouldn't even let me into his room," Ginger said. "I had to talk to him through his closed door. He just laughed and told me to come back when I had a check with me."

I had to ask. "Are you sure it was Duncan's voice you heard?"

Ginger's mouth opened, and she gasped like a fish before she asked, "Who else would it have been?"

A sudden idea came to me. "You said that you and Greg received separate letters, and you talked about two separate appointments, but then you told us Duncan set your appointments for the same time. Can you be more clear about this?"

I knew I was being unrealistic when I asked Ginger to make things clear, but she did her best. "We had separate appointments at first. One at six and one at seven," Ginger explained. "Then Duncan telephoned and asked that Greg and I come together. So we did." She pouted as she said, "He was such a grouch. I mean, he wanted us to come separately. Then he wanted us together. Then he complained that I was supposed to come at six. Fuss, fuss, fuss. Honestly! I mean—"

I couldn't help interrupting. "Did you and Greg bring the original letters he sent you?"

"No," Ginger said, and Greg shook his head.

Walter Hampton put a protective arm around his mother. "Go to your room and rest," he told her. "Since they won't allow you to leave, I'll check into the hotel so I can be on hand to help you." He tossed his car keys to me. "I'd like to register. My luggage is in the red sports coupe parked near the front door. Take care of it."

Dad says, "Always be polite," I kept telling myself as I walked to the desk, but it was difficult. I asked Keisha to take care of registering Hampton. I took his luggage from his car and carried both pieces into the hotel. The black overnight case caught my eye. There was a sticker on it that I recognized. The motel down the road slapped those stickers on their guests' luggage as a kind of advertising. "I stayed at Mountain Motel," the sticker read. I was confused as I watched Hampton take his key. How did he get a sticker from Mountain Motel on his suitcase?

Before I could ask, I found myself surrounded. Bev Parker and three of her girlfriends came running through the open front door of the hotel. Bev is Lew's daughter, and she just turned fourteen last month. When I saw the crowd of teenagers, I remembered that Lew helped with his church's youth group. Bev ran up and gave me a hug. Her eyes were red from crying, and I got a sinking feeling. Were they here to tell me bad news?

CHAPTER 9

I held Bev Parker's shoulders and studied her tear-streaked face. "How is your dad?" I asked.

Bev sniffled and said, "The doctor told us it was only a concussion. Mom's with him, but they wouldn't let the rest of us stay."

I sighed with relief. "Is someone with your mother?"

Bev nodded. "Lily Chan."

"Good. Lily will take good care of her. How long will your dad be in the clinic?" I asked.

Bev and her friends tried to answer at the same time, but Bev's voice was louder. "He has to stay until he knows where he is. Dad talked to Mom, but he thought it was yesterday and he'd been playing touch football with his brother."

I smiled. I didn't think Lew's confusion would last long. He had to be doing well since he was awake and talking.

But worry darkened Bev's eyes. "I heard one of the medics tell someone that Dad was attacked because he knew who killed that man here in the hotel. Is that true?"

I answered as fully as I could. "Your dad told me that he'd seen someone leaving Duncan Tyler's room, but he didn't know who it was."

"Are you sure that's all he said?" Bev asked. "Officer Morgan is making a policeman stay in Dad's room all the time."

The girls were suddenly quiet, waiting for information.

"I don't know why someone hurt your father, Bev," I said.

Bev grumbled, "Dad should never have told anyone anything he saw."

I tried to explain. "He would have been in danger even if he never talked about it. Because he told me what he'd seen, we have a better chance to catch the person who committed the murder."

Just then Gran came out of her office. "Bev," she cried, "how's your father?"

Bev ran to her and got another hug. Bev's friends followed her, all answering Gran's question at the same time. I knew Gran would take good care of the girls. So I rolled the luggage cart toward the elevators.

Walter Hampton waited there, tapping his foot impatiently. Ginger was nowhere in sight, but as the elevator doors opened, Greg hurried up and stepped into the elevator with Hampton and me.

We rode up to the third floor. Greg didn't go directly to his room. He stood in front of the ice machine while I put Hampton's luggage in his room and went through the routine of showing him how to work the heat and air conditioner controls. Hampton didn't offer to give me a tip. Scowling, he plopped down by the phone and ignored me, so I left.

As I shut Hampton's door, Greg stopped me. "Would you mind if I asked you a couple of questions?" he asked.

"Go ahead. I'll try to answer them."

"I've been wondering." He paused before going on. "I need to know. How strong is your roof?"

The question surprised me so much all I could do was repeat, "My roof?"

"I mean, you get all that snow in the winter," he said. "The roof is pitched to make the snow run off, but doesn't some of it freeze up there and weaken the roof? What if it fell in?"

"That won't happen," I answered. "We have the roof examined every spring. We fix any problems while they're small."

Greg didn't give up. "But what if Silver Ridge got a lot more snow than usual?"

"If there was enough snow to make the situation dangerous, we'd close the hotel," I said. "Why are you—?"

"You wouldn't have time to close the hotel if there was an avalanche," he insisted.

"You want to use this information in a story. Right?" I asked. As Greg nodded, I said, "Then why don't you talk to my uncle Jim? He'll show you how the hotel was built and tell you everything you want to know about mountain snow. Let's go down to the desk and ask for him."

When we got on the elevator, I kept the empty luggage cart between us. I didn't trust any of the writers.

At the front desk, Keisha sent for Uncle Jim. She then told me that Eddie Jackson wanted to see me as soon as possible. Eddie is the head chef at the Silver Ridge Hotel.

I left Greg to wait for Jim and hurried to the kitchen. Eddie put down a long stirring spoon as I came in and asked, "Stacy, can you tell me how Lew is doing?"

I told Eddie what I had learned from Bev and what Lew had told me earlier.

Eddie frowned. "Lew didn't tell me about seeing someone leave the room."

"At the time he must not have thought it was important. Lew didn't know that Tyler had been killed until he came to work this morning."

Eddie picked up the spoon again and stirred something in the largest pot. I could tell by the beefy fragrance that he was making French onion soup. He sniffed it deeply, nodded with satisfaction, then turned back to me. "Last night Lew did tell me something else, though. I don't know if it means anything, Stacy, but it's weird. So I'll pass it on to you. After Lew brought the champagne to Lady Jane Hampton, he told me she'd given him a large tip. She had laughed and told him it was 'in honor of bright relief.'"

"'Bright relief'? That doesn't make sense."

"It didn't to Lew and me, either. But then I got to thinking. Sometimes people do or say strange things when they want to be noticed and remembered. What if Lady Hampton killed Mr. Tyler? What if she wanted Lew to be her alibi? He could say what time he saw her in her own room if she said something crazy. He'd remember that."

I said, "Ramon and Morgan think that the murderer might have tried to kill Lew to keep him from talking about something he knew. If Lady Jane was the murderer and wanted Lew to be her alibi, she wouldn't have hit him."

Eddie leaned forward and lowered his voice. "I think one of the other suspects went after Lew to keep him from protecting Lady Jane."

"That would mean someone else would know she committed the murder." I shook my head. "No. That's too complicated."

Eddie shrugged. "That may be what you think, Stacy, but I might be right. I just want you to pass the word on to Ramon."

"I'll tell him," I said. Eddie looked so intent, I smiled and added, "I know if I don't, you'll make me come in here and chop vegetables all day."

Eddie smiled back. "It would do you good to work in the kitchen," he said. "Chopping vegetables keeps you from getting tense. Maybe you should think about training to take over my job here next year when I open my own restaurant. You might like being a chef better than being a security chief."

I had no desire to chop vegetables. "I'll go talk to Ramon right now," I told Eddie.

I went to the ballroom, but it was empty, and the police had sealed it with tape. *Maybe Ramon's in my office*, I thought, so I headed in that direction.

I heard a slight sound in the hall behind me and whirled around. But no one was there. Before I opened the office door, I nervously glanced over my shoulder. Even the lobby was empty and quiet. Perhaps Eddie was right and I needed to work in the kitchen. I was getting jumpy. I even imagined someone was watching me.

I walked into my empty office and wondered where Ramon and Morgan had gone. The sticker on Walter Hampton's luggage bothered me, so I picked up the phone. Before Ramon and Morgan came back, I might be able to get some answers. I dialed the number of the Mountain Motel and got Elena, who's often at the main desk.

"Hi, Elena," I said. "This is Stacy Champagne. Can you

tell me if a Walter Hampton stayed with you last night?"

"He sure did," Elena said. "I hope he didn't check into the Silver Ridge. I wouldn't wish a guy like that on anybody. Biggest complainer I ever met."

"I noticed," I said, "and he *is* here. I need some information about him. What time did he arrive at your motel?"

"Let me check," Elena said. I could hear the clicking of her computer keyboard. Then she told me, "Mr. Hampton checked in yesterday afternoon at five-fifteen. He didn't make any phone calls. He paid in full this morning when he checked out. He paid cash. There isn't anything else on the computer about him."

"You told me what I need to know," I said. "Thanks, Elena."

As I hung up the phone I wondered, *Why had Hampton stayed in Silver Ridge last night? Why didn't he come to our hotel where his mother was staying? Why didn't he tell anyone that he was in town?* I stood up and walked to the window while I tried to figure out Walter Hampton.

I don't know what made me notice, but suddenly I felt as if someone were behind me. Was that soft sound I heard the door being opened?

I swung around, but there wasn't anyone else in the room. I glanced at the door. It was open a crack. But I remembered pulling it closed. Was someone spying on me? I quietly edged close to the door. I grabbed the handle and swung it open.

CHAPTER
10

Out at the front desk, Keisha turned and looked at me. "What are you doing?" she asked.

I walked to the desk and said quietly, "Someone was at my office door. Did you see who it was?"

Keisha shook her head. "I wasn't watching the office area. I was talking with Ginger Gage. She wanted to know if we were snowbound, how long we'd have food to eat—before we ate each other." Keisha chuckled. "These writers sure ask strange questions."

I glanced around the lobby. Why did I still feel jumpy? What was the matter with me? The lobby was quiet and practically deserted, as it usually was on a late Saturday afternoon. Most guests go shopping or hiking on Saturdays when the weather is beautiful. Was someone aware of this? Or did someone think I would be somewhere else and my office would be empty?

A thought struck me. Keisha hadn't been watching the

office area because Ginger had been busy asking her questions. Could Greg and Ginger be working together? While Ginger was the lookout, Greg could get into the office. What was he after? The answer was easy. He wanted the award check that was sitting in the safe. Were Greg and Ginger the thieves who took the check last year?

Dad arrived, carrying a room service tray. As he held it out, he said, "This is for you, Stacy. Your grandmother's taking a nap, and I want you to have some lunch."

"Thanks, Dad. I forgot all about lunch. I wanted to keep watch over the safe," I said. I lifted the cover from the plate and saw thin, golden strips of grilled chicken on top of a garden salad. I could smell Eddie's famous raspberry-pecan salad dressing. I suddenly became very hungry.

Dad and I walked back to my office. I cleared off part of my desk so he could put the tray there. Then I told him about my feeling that someone had tried to come into the office or maybe had been spying on me.

He frowned as he thought. "Are you sure that when you opened the door, no one was there?" he asked.

"That's right," I told him. I realized I shouldn't have worried him. "It was probably just my imagination." I quickly changed the subject by telling him what Ginger had asked.

Dad smiled and said, "I think writers look at the world in a different way."

It wasn't just writers. I thought of how Amy had caused me to take another look at my dad. "You've worked at Silver Ridge all your life," I said. "Do you still enjoy it?"

He looked surprised but began to answer. Unfortunately, he was interrupted by a knock at the door. It opened and Ramon and Morgan walked in. My dad patted my hand and left. I was disappointed. I had hoped he'd open up and I'd have a chance to understand him better.

"Look at that chicken salad," Morgan said. "I told you she'd get a better lunch than we did."

Ramon shrugged. "That was great French onion soup." He smiled at me. "Eddie Jackson fed us soup and crackers while he talked to us. He went over what he told you about the strange remark Lady Hampton said to Lew. Then he gave us his idea about who committed the murder."

Morgan sat in my chair and spun a pen on the edge of the desk. "Eddie's idea doesn't work. If Lady Jane killed Duncan Tyler, then who did Lew see leaving Tyler's room? Whoever had been in the room would have known Tyler was dead and would have called the police—unless he was the killer."

"How about Lady Jane's son?" I asked. I told them about his stay at the nearby Mountain Motel.

Morgan looked at Ramon. "Hampton didn't tell us that he was in Silver Ridge last night."

Ramon thought it over. "He does have a dark, navy blue coat and a hat. We'd better talk with the people at the motel." He turned to me. "What name did he use there?"

"His own," I answered.

Morgan didn't look happy about that. "Stacy, are you sure? He wouldn't use his own name if he planned to kill someone."

"Maybe he didn't plan to kill Duncan," I said. "Maybe he thought he could talk Duncan out of blackmailing Lady Jane. Hampton has a bad disposition and a quick temper. He might have lost his temper, picked up the wine bottle, and hit Duncan." As Morgan and Ramon thought about what I'd said, I added, "He could have tried to get rid of Lew the same way, by hitting him in the head with that heavy vase."

Morgan jumped up. "Let's have a talk with Walter Hampton," he told Ramon.

"Wait. There's something else," I said. I told them

about someone opening my office door. "I wonder if someone was after the award check."

"That would be a stupid thing to do when there are police in the hotel," Morgan said.

Ramon rubbed his chin as he thought. "Amy told us that Ginger and Greg sat across from her at the dinner last year. Maybe Ginger distracted everyone while Greg took the check out of the briefcase."

"No. He'd have had to climb under the table to reach the briefcase," Morgan said impatiently. "Let's work on the murder here in Silver Ridge. Forget about what happened to that check last year. That's just wasting time."

"I don't agree," I said stubbornly. "The murder might have been tied in with the award checks."

Morgan's face began to turn red. Ramon quickly said, "We need to give more thought to that manuscript. It has to be hidden somewhere. It would help our investigation if we could find and read it."

"If Hampton took the manuscript, he could have dumped it nearly anywhere in Silver Ridge," Morgan said. "We could waste a lot of man hours searching for it, and I don't think we're ever going to find it."

I knew that Morgan might be right. The manuscript could be anywhere. But what if it were still in our hotel? I knew all the corners and spots to hide things. After all, I had grown up in the hotel. When I was a child, as a game I wrote secret messages and hid them around the hotel. Some of them might still be in their secret hiding places. As I thought about those messages, I began to get excited. Maybe the game I'd played could help me find the manuscript.

I couldn't begin my hunt until Uncle Jim returned to the hotel. I put him in charge of guarding the office safe, then took an elevator to the third floor. The elevator was empty, which gave me a few seconds to go over the floor and walls. I didn't really expect to find manuscript pages tucked under the rug or jammed in the emergency phone box—favorite hiding places in my past. Now I was looking for pages in a manuscript that would be a larger package than my small, secret notes.

The third floor was quiet when I got off the elevator. For a moment I felt a chill, remembering the silence when I'd been waiting with Duncan Tyler's body. Then I heard voices and a faint melody from the television in someone's room, and I relaxed.

Most people who looked down the empty hallway would not have believed there was any place in which to hide something. I knew better. I began with the area in front of the elevator. The carpet was still tight around the elevator. No one could lift a section to hide something under it. There was a small table between the two elevators. The large vase of artificial flowers on it reminded me of the even larger vase that someone had used to hit Lew. I was determined to find that person. I pulled the flowers out of the vase and peered inside, but the vase was empty. I stuck the flowers back and opened the drawer in the table. Nothing was hidden in it.

I walked slowly along the hall. The first door on my left was Lady Jane's. As I stood outside the doorway, I could hear the television in her room. I decided she was watching a sports show, because the announcer was giving a rapid description of a horse race.

Lew had stood in this spot when he saw someone leaving Duncan Tyler's room. I looked in both directions and could see the entire hallway clearly. Standing where Lew had stood, I realized something new. Lew said he only saw the person from the back. To get to the elevators, the person would have had to walk past Lew. He would have seen the person's face if he—or she—had taken the elevator. That meant that Lew had seen someone walking away from Duncan's room, farther down the hall. Now I had a better idea of where to hunt for the manuscript.

I examined closely the part of the hall past Duncan's room. I couldn't find any loose spots in the carpet. The walls were smooth—no hiding places there. Along each wall there were several framed photographs of our hotel in its early years. I took each photo down and examined the backing. I didn't find a single manuscript page.

I was replacing the last photo on the wall when I heard the sound of a door opening. I glanced up, but the hall was still empty. All of the doors seemed to be shut, but one must have been opened a crack because again I felt as if I were being watched. Self-consciously, I swept the top of the frame with my hand as though I were wiping away some dust.

What was wrong with me? Why did I keep thinking I was being watched? I knew I should march back down the hall. If all the doors were closed, then I'd know how silly this feeling was. I knew what I should do, but I couldn't make myself do it.

Instead, I headed in the opposite direction to the stairwell. I managed to walk normally. If I were being watched, I wouldn't let anyone know how nervous I felt. I opened the door to the stairs, and the door squeaked. I made a mental note to have the hinges oiled, but I was so frightened, I was having trouble keeping my thoughts in order. I ran down the stairs as fast as I could.

I was two steps from the second floor when I heard the squeak of the third-floor door again. Someone had opened it. Someone was coming after me.

CHAPTER 11

I skipped over stairs and jumped down to the landing. I hopped down the last set of stairs and flung myself at the door to the lobby. I raced through it, and stopped instantly when I looked up to see Dad standing at the reception desk.

He gave me a surprised look. "Is everything all right, Stacy?" he asked.

"I—I think so," I said. Now that I was standing in the lobby, I couldn't believe someone had been following me. My imagination had to be working overtime.

I decided that a guest on the third floor must have chosen to walk down the stairs instead of taking the elevator. Fitness nuts often ignored the elevators in favor of the stairs. At any second someone would open the door, and I'd feel foolish for letting myself get scared. I waited to see who would come through the door from the stairs.

The door didn't open.

Even someone who was walking very slowly down the stairs would have had enough time to reach the lobby. I walked over to the door, took a deep breath, and forced myself to open it. The stairs were empty.

I listened carefully, but I couldn't hear a sound. I let the door swing closed and thought about what had happened. I had heard the door from the third floor open behind me. I was sure about that. No one from the third floor would have any reason to stop at the second floor. Maybe someone had started down the stairs, then had remembered something left behind, and had gone back to his room. That made sense. I tried to make myself think clearly, but the nervous feeling wouldn't go away.

Dad suddenly looked from his work back to me. "I'm sorry, Stacy. My mind was on a reservation that just arrived. I should have told you right away. Amy Prescott's grandfather, Mr. Joshua Prescott, arrived a few minutes ago. Ramon is talking to him in your office, and Ramon wants you to join them."

Glad to get my mind off the stalker in the stairwell, I strode down the short hall and entered my office.

Joshua Prescott sat on the uncomfortable sofa with Amy. He gripped her hand. I'm sure he had been worried about her. Morgan sat at the desk, and Ramon stood, leaning against the wall. Mr. Prescott was a tall man with a sense of authority we all seemed to feel. I could see why Amy found it hard to tell him her ideas.

"You're asking if Duncan has been blackmailing me?" Mr. Prescott said in surprise to Ramon as I entered the room. He stopped speaking and turned toward me as Ramon introduced me.

After learning that I was the hotel's security chief and had a right to be there, Mr. Prescott answered Ramon's question. "No, Duncan was not blackmailing me."

Amy broke in. "Grandfather, how could Duncan possibly think you'd print a book that would tell secrets about the other writers?"

Mr. Prescott patted Amy's hand. "He knew better than that. I'm afraid that Duncan was simply trying an old—and not very honest—writers' trick."

"Trick? What do you mean—trick?" Morgan asked.

"I have a standard contract with all my writers," Mr. Prescott explained. "When I offer a contract to a writer, I put an option clause in the contract. That means I have the right to publish the next book by that writer. If I turn down the next manuscript submitted by the writer, then he's free to sell it to some other publisher.

"I should point out that for the last two years Duncan won the award for selling the most books." Mr. Prescott added, "However, the book he wrote this year didn't sell as well. Duncan blamed me and thought I should have spent more on advertising for the book."

Amy interrupted. "Would more advertising have helped it?" In spite of what she had told me, I could see that the details of the family business seemed important to her.

"I don't think so," Mr. Prescott answered. "Duncan wrote about a crime that was no longer of interest to many readers."

Morgan fidgeted. "What does all that have to do with a writers' trick?"

"Duncan had to offer me his next manuscript," Mr. Prescott said. "If he wrote a book that was so bad I'd be forced to turn it down, then he'd be free to write another manuscript and submit it to another publishing house." He slowly shook his head. "Fortunately that trick is rarely done, but Duncan wouldn't be above trying it."

"You're telling us that Duncan knew you wouldn't publish the manuscript," Ramon said. "He put in the embarrassing details about the other authors so you would have to turn it down. Is that right?"

"It very well could be, from what you've told me," Mr. Prescott said. "As you know, I haven't seen the manuscript."

Ramon had another question. "One of the writers gave Tyler a large sum of money so that he'd drop a chapter from the book. Why would she do that unless she thought you would really print the book?"

Mr. Prescott frowned. "There is no telling what Duncan threatened. I doubt if what he told her had anything to do with the truth."

"Did Tyler have debts? Any money problems?" Ramon asked.

Amy said, "I can answer that. Duncan's girlfriend supported him so he could write full time. He didn't have another job."

Mr. Prescott sighed. "Duncan was a bright young man. His problem was that he thought he was smarter than most people, and he made his feelings known."

Amy's mouth turned down in disgust. "Duncan was acting more smug than I'd ever seen him," she said. "I thought it was because he was sure he'd get the award again."

"I don't think so, considering how poorly Duncan's latest book was doing," her grandfather said. "The writers keep a close watch on how well their books are selling. I wouldn't be surprised if all of them guess long before the award weekend if they're likely to win or not."

That gave me something to think about. Maybe Lady Jane was sure she would win on Friday night and had ordered the champagne to celebrate a little ahead of time. Maybe when she talked to Lew about "bright relief" she meant how she'd feel getting the award.

Mr. Prescott spoke firmly. "I'm sorry that Duncan tried to fool me and blackmail the other authors. He had a fine mind, but he obviously didn't have a sense of honor."

Morgan spoke up. "Tell us about the other writers. In your opinion, were any of them likely to react to blackmail by murdering Duncan?"

Mr. Prescott leaned back against the sofa. "I can't believe any of them killed Duncan."

"There were no signs of a struggle at the scene," Ramon told him. "Duncan must have let the murderer into his room and sat at his desk with him. I don't think he'd behave that way with a stranger."

"What about someone on the hotel staff?" Amy asked. "They have keys to get into the rooms. Duncan wouldn't have thought that anyone from the hotel would harm him."

She was blaming the hotel staff again! Ramon gave me a warning glance, so I clenched my teeth to keep from saying anything.

"We considered that too," Ramon said. "But we're pretty sure that someone searched Duncan's room and took something from inside the dresser. Since we found a few sheets of what was probably his manuscript on the floor, we suspect that the manuscript is what was taken. I doubt if someone from the hotel would have stolen a manuscript and left thousands of dollars in cash on the victim."

Amy didn't look convinced, but her grandfather gave Ramon a serious look. "I can see why you suspect the writers," he said. "But from what you told me, I don't see how any of them could take Duncan's threats seriously."

"I disagree," Ramon said. "Greg and Ginger Gage could

lose their contract with the perfume company if it were known that Ginger had been having an affair."

"Possibly," Mr. Prescott admitted. "The perfume company hopes to advertise the two of them as a symbol of the perfect, romantic couple."

"Did that contract put them into a financial position where they could pay a great deal of money to Tyler?" Ramon asked.

Mr. Prescott shook his head. "Not at this time," he said. "Duncan must have known they couldn't give him anything until they received payment from the perfume company."

"What about the other writers?" Morgan asked. "Do you know if they'd be able to pay Tyler?"

"Clara would," Mr. Prescott said. "She has a teaching job, a savings plan, retirement benefits—everything. But count her out as a possible murderer. Clara is a very nervous person, afraid of her own shadow. She's not a killer type.

"Lady Jane's family is well-off, so she could pay Duncan if she wanted to," Mr. Prescott continued. "You've met her, so you know she has a mind of her own. I don't think she would give in to blackmail. At the same time, I'm sure she wouldn't kill Duncan—or anyone else."

He thought a moment, then said, "Mark tends to move from job to job. He spends his money as soon as he gets it, so I don't think he could come up with blackmail money."

"Mark Bannon could still be the killer," Morgan said.

Mr. Prescott shook his head in disagreement again. "You've met Mark. He takes life in a lighthearted way. If Duncan wrote an entire book about Mark's flirting and drinking, Mark would simply be flattered."

"What about Lady Hampton's son, Walter?" Morgan said.

Remembering Walter Hampton's temper, I could see why Morgan asked. I could easily picture Walter hitting Duncan in a burst of anger. And he might very well have lain in wait for Lew.

"Walter does have a temper," Mr. Prescott said. "He shouts. He threatens. I've even seen him kick a door. But I don't think he's ever hit a person in his life."

Mr. Prescott put his head into his hands for a moment. Then he looked up. "I'd like to help you catch the person who killed Duncan, but I can't believe it was one of my writers. I feel disloyal talking about them with you."

He might have said more, but he was interrupted. Keisha ran into the office.

"Stacy!" she said. "Come quick. We have a security problem!"

CHAPTER 12

Ramon stood up. Morgan was ready to join me, but Keisha shook her head. "A guest in the coffee shop broke some dishes. Alicia tried to calm her, but the guest is upset. We just need Stacy."

When I entered the coffee shop I could see the mess. The staff was quickly cleaning it up, but it looked as if a whole tray of food had crashed onto the floor.

Ginger stood by her chair. Tears streaked her makeup. "I didn't mean to bump into the waiter," Ginger said. "Greg had me so upset that when I jumped up I wasn't looking. I'll be glad to pay for the dishes that got broken."

I tried to reassure her. "It was an accident. The hotel doesn't expect you to pay."

"Oh, thank goodness," Ginger said. She sighed with relief.

Were Greg and Ginger so short of funds an extra expense would frighten her? I wondered how they'd have the money to pay blackmail. Or had they already paid it?

Greg looked up at Ginger. "If you had stayed here and dealt with the problem, you wouldn't have bumped into anyone."

Ginger's voice rose. "Dealt with what problem? Clara's silly ideas? No one can prove that I had an affair with Duncan."

What was Ginger saying? That she hadn't had an affair? Or that no one could prove she'd had an affair? Those were two very different things.

"You kissed him!" Greg snapped.

"That was last year at the award dinner. I just gave him a kiss because he'd won."

Greg's scowl grew deeper. "You didn't kiss Lady Jane when she won this year."

"I didn't feel like it. She's always rude to me," Ginger said. "Look, I admit I flirted with Duncan, but just in a fun way. That's all anyone can say about me."

Greg didn't answer her. He turned to me and said, "Please sit down, Stacy. We need a third party to help us solve our problem."

Ginger surprised me. "Yes. Please sit with us. You can help." She pushed a chair toward me and took her own seat.

I didn't want to join them. I'm not a marriage counselor. But this was a chance to understand Greg and Ginger better. Maybe I'd even find out something that would help solve the murder. I sat down.

Greg leaned forward. "Ever since Ginger openly kissed Duncan last year, Lady Jane has been giving me hints. Yesterday she came right out and said that Ginger was crazy about Duncan."

Ginger sniffed. "Don't you see? That was her way of getting even. She's been angry with me ever since I reviewed her last year's mystery for one of the mystery magazines. The story was full of holes and totally unbelievable, and I said so. She didn't like the fact that I had to tell the truth about it."

Truth? Or jealousy? I wondered.

Greg studied his wife as if he were trying to believe her. "But if you weren't spending time with Duncan, where were you yesterday before the award dinner? I couldn't find you anywhere."

"I was on the terrace, watching the beautiful sunset," Ginger said. "You and I usually watch them together, so I hoped you'd receive my mental messages and join me."

Greg leaned back in his chair. "I should have known that's where you'd be. I've been a fool."

Ginger smiled tenderly. "Yes, you have, my love. How could you be so jealous?"

Greg took her hand and kissed her fingertips. "Do you know I even tried to cover for your absence when I thought you were with Duncan? I pointed out the time and told Jim Champagne that you were in our room, still getting dressed."

I nearly blurted out a protest. Ginger had been outside Duncan's room around seven. Lady Jane had seen her. Had Lady Jane been lying about that too? Or was Ginger lying?

Ginger began making kissy lips at Greg. I couldn't stand much more of this, so I broke in. "Was Duncan blackmailing you?"

"He tried to," Greg said, "but we wouldn't give in."

"He even told us he'd written a legal agreement," Ginger said. "Can you imagine—legal blackmail? We refused to sign it, no matter how much he needed the money."

I asked, "Did Duncan have money problems?"

"Oh, yes," Ginger answered. "Ever since he broke up with his girlfriend last year."

"Where is this legal agreement?" I asked.

Both Greg and Ginger looked blank. "We didn't even see it," Ginger said.

Greg got to his feet. "Let's not think about Duncan anymore, my darling. Those thoughts are making us both unhappy."

"You're right, dearest," Ginger said. She stood, still clinging to his hand, and looked down at me. "I suppose you have to tell your friend, Ramon, about our conversation," she said. "Just please don't say a word to Lady Jane."

As they left the coffee shop, I had the strong feeling that they'd just played a scene for my benefit. That was certainly a phony argument. They wanted me to take information to Ramon and tell him what I had heard and what I believed. Well, I wasn't going to fall for it.

I was leaving the coffee shop when I was stopped by a shout. "Stacy! We heard you had another murder!" I looked around, embarrassed. The coffee shop was almost empty except for four of our Silver Ridge residents—Millie, Jack, Tess, and Glenna Sutton.

They were all dressed up and seemed very excited. Elderly Mrs. Sutton was wearing a blue and scarlet caftan with huge dangle earrings. Jack wore a shirt and tie under a red, out-of-season Christmas vest that was at least a size too tight. Tess wore a green leather skirt that must have shrunk. Does leather shrink? And Millie was arrayed in the black, bustled, 1890s dress she wore in her job at Silver Ridge's historical museum. All four of them looked as curious as kids who were about to open birthday presents.

"We came to get a look at the authors," Glenna yelled at me. "Authors being eccentric, as everybody knows."

Eccentric as the foursome who came to spy on them? I nearly choked, I tried so hard not to laugh. "I think you'll find them to be very normal people," I said.

Millie leaned forward and whispered, "How could they be normal? They're writers, aren't they?"

"Yes, but—"

Jack spoke out of one side of his mouth. "And one of them's a killer."

My cell phone rang, so I unclipped it from my belt and answered it. It was easier than dealing with our local celebrity hunters.

"Mr. Prescott asked to talk to you. He's in his room," Keisha told me.

I made note of his room number. Third floor. I was uncomfortable about taking the elevator there. *Don't be silly*, I told myself. *Nothing else is going to happen.* I excused myself and forced myself to get on the elevator.

The number in the elevator flashed "three." I stepped out of the elevator and onto the third floor. It was then I heard a horrible, chilling wail.

My stomach flipped over. I ran in the direction of Clara's room, from where the wail seemed to come, and pulled out my passkeys. Without even knocking, I opened the door.

Clara stood alone by the table. The telephone lay on the floor, and Clara was weeping. I was thankful that I hadn't found another body.

Someone brushed my shoulder, and I jumped, spinning around.

"Well, Clara, it's obvious that you've been talking with your fiancé," Lady Jane said. She pushed past me and entered Clara's room.

I stepped inside and shut the door behind me. "What's going on?" I asked. "Why did you call out?"

Clara dropped to the end of the bed and covered her face with her hands. Her sobbing grew louder.

"Sit down please, Stacy," Lady Jane said. "I think I can tell you what happened." She sat next to Clara and handed her a lace-edged handkerchief.

"My life is over," Clara managed to say. "Mitchell said that Duncan ruined my life. He said I'll lose my job and my reputation when the school finds out I wrote Duncan's—and other people's—term papers."

"Nonsense," Lady Jane said. "Who's going to tell them? Mitchell?"

Clara stopped crying and stared at Lady Jane. "Mitchell would never do that," she said.

Lady Jane raised an eyebrow. It was clear she didn't think very highly of Mitchell. "I don't want to be unfair to him," she said. "Did he tell you that you could count on his help during this difficult time?"

Clara looked embarrassed. "No, he didn't. He wants to break our engagement."

"That sounds like the selfish, self-centered Mitchell Foster I know," Lady Jane said.

"You don't really know him," Clara protested in a weak voice.

Lady Jane spoke firmly. "I understand people well. I've met Mitchell's kind before, and I expect very little of him."

"Mitchell pointed out to me that he has to put his career first," Clara said.

I was puzzled. I had understood that Mitchell had broken their engagement a few weeks ago. If that was so, then why was Clara so upset about it now?

"Why didn't Mitchell come with you this weekend as he had originally planned?" I asked her.

Lady Jane looked surprised. "Mitchell was coming? I'm glad he changed his plans. We were spared having him around all weekend."

Clara spoke directly to me. "When I got the letter from Duncan, I asked Mitchell not to come. I was terrified to have Mitchell know I was being blackmailed."

"But you just told him," Lady Jane said.

"I wanted to be open and truthful. A marriage should be based on trust." Clara's voice trembled, and she shuddered. "I guess I was wrong."

I didn't want Clara to begin sobbing again, so I quickly asked, "What happened at your appointment with Duncan Tyler?"

"He offered me wine. I turned it down. I had closed my savings account. I brought cash—as Duncan wanted. I handed him the money, and he gave me Chapter Three of his manuscript. He promised there were no other copies."

I was startled. I knew the police had searched her room for the manuscript. Why didn't Ramon tell me that Clara was in possession of part of the missing manuscript? "Where is Chapter Three now?" I asked her.

"I tore all six pages into little, tiny scraps of paper," she said. "Then I threw them away in the dumpster behind the hotel."

"Did you read the chapter?"

"Yes," Clara answered. "Duncan had done just what he'd threatened to do. He'd written about the term paper business I'd set up." She sniffled. "He made me look like such a cheat. It really wasn't like that. Well, it was, but it wasn't."

"I can't believe you gave in to Duncan's blackmail," Lady Jane said impatiently.

"You don't understand," Clara told her. "Your problem wasn't as terrible. You wouldn't be ruined if people learned you weren't on good terms with the Queen."

"That's not—" Lady Jane began to say, then stopped.

"Go on," I suggested. "That's not what?"

"Never mind about me. We're here to help Clara," Lady Jane said. "We can't change what happened, but we can take action for the future."

Clara put her hands over her face again. "I don't have much of a future," she said.

"Of course you do. If Mitchell *does* leak the information to your superiors at the school where you both teach, you have other options. Your books are popular and they sell well. Quit your teaching job and write full time."

"But if people know what I've done . . ."

"If your readers love your characters and stories, they'll forgive anything," Lady Jane said.

"And Mitchell will forgive me too." Clara actually smiled at Lady Jane.

I was glad Clara felt better, but I couldn't forget how unhappy she had been. Until Lady Jane gave her a new purpose, Clara had actually believed that Duncan could destroy her life. I left the room feeling uneasy. Clara had a powerful motive to kill Duncan to save her job and her future marriage.

CHAPTER
13

Amy looked concerned as she opened the door to her grandfather's room. "I thought I heard someone cry out a few minutes ago," she said. "Do you know who it was?"

"Yes, but it's nothing to worry about," I answered. "The problem has been taken care of."

We joined Joshua Prescott, who sat in an armchair by the window.

Amy said, "I was supposed to drive the writers back to Denver tomorrow after lunch. But Officer Morgan said we'd have to stay while he continues the investigation. Do you know how long we'll be here?"

"I'll check with Officer Morgan. Then I'll let you know," I told her.

Amy sighed. "I want this weekend to be over," she said. "These writers' weekends are bad enough. Driving the writers back and forth to Denver isn't easy either."

Mr. Prescott frowned at her. "You never told me that you disliked these weekends. You should have said something."

I could tell that Amy wished she hadn't spoken her mind. She twisted her fingers together and took a deep breath before she said, "Last year Mark sat in my office worrying aloud that he might get carsick. He wanted me to leave and get him some pills for motion sickness that very minute. I finally grew so tired of his complaints that I went to the nearest health food store. I bought him pills for motion sickness and candied ginger to munch on. Then he insisted on sitting right behind me in the van. He insisted that the spot behind the driver is the safest. All the way to Boulder he told me one stupid joke after another." She sighed. "Even so, he wasn't the worst passenger in the lot."

I spoke without thinking. "Who could have been worse than that?"

"Clara," Amy answered. "Coming back, she sat behind me. She didn't think I could drive without her help. I not only got her constant backseat advice, I had to deal with her gasps and squeals of fright every time a truck passed us or I changed lanes."

Mr. Prescott spoke slowly. "I had no idea you hated the writers' weekends so much."

Amy looked both guilty and sorry she had spoken out. "I shouldn't complain, Grandfather. You're right. I should have told you how I felt after the first weekend."

"Meeting with writers has always been one of my favorite parts of the publishing business," Mr. Prescott told her. "They're always curious, and they always have such fresh, interesting ideas."

I began to think that Amy *was* in the wrong business. Her grandfather's viewpoint was very different from her own.

Amy kept trying to make up for her outburst. "The writers weren't as troublesome this year," she said quietly. "Mark is taking a new medicine to prevent motion sickness. And coming up here to Silver Ridge, Ginger sat behind me. She spent most of the time asking me questions about the sales and marketing side of the business."

"Ginger has brought up some good ideas about increasing sales," Mr. Prescott agreed.

"I've found that I like the sales side of the business better than the editorial side," Amy said. "Could we talk about that, Grandfather? If it's all right with you, I think that I'd like to work in the sales department."

He nodded and said, "I'd planned on training you in the sales department. I want you to become familiar with every division in our publishing house."

I was glad that Amy had found a way to solve her problem with the family business, but I still had some questions that needed answers. "Could I ask you about the award dinner last year?" I said. "Did Greg or Ginger do anything unusual during the dinner?"

Amy looked surprised. Then she laughed. "Yes," she said. "As you've heard, when I announced that Duncan was the winner, Ginger jumped up and kissed him."

"Could Greg have stolen the check while everyone was looking at Ginger?"

"No," Amy said. "The envelope was still in my hands, unopened."

"How about *before* the check was awarded?" I asked. "Did anyone spill a glass of water? Make a scene? Have an argument?"

"No. Nothing like that happened," Amy insisted. "In fact, everyone was in a cheerful mood. I remember that we had fun discussing the latest movies."

I didn't give up. "Did anyone drop a napkin? Or have to climb under the table to pick up a fork?"

Amy shook her head. "I told you. Everything went smoothly."

"Until you discovered that the check was missing," Mr. Prescott said.

"After that, the weekend fell apart," Amy admitted. "I didn't get any sleep. The police searched our rooms—not finishing until close to midnight. Then, around two A.M., Clara thought she heard someone trying to break in her window, so she telephoned my room and woke me up."

"Didn't you call hotel security?" I asked.

"Of course," Amy answered. "But they couldn't find anything. I think it was Clara's imagination." She sighed. "Then a little before six, Mark woke me up. He had left his shaving kit in the van and needed me to unlock the van so he could get the kit. I was exhausted."

I knew how she felt. I'd been up late helping with the murder investigation, and I was worn out. At least Gran had let me sleep late this morning.

There was nothing more I could learn from the Prescotts, so I left Mr. Prescott's room. While I waited for the elevator, I got the odd feeling again that someone was watching me. I knew I was being silly, but I couldn't make myself turn around to look down the hall behind me.

As the elevator door opened, I nervously jumped into the elevator. Keeeping my hand by the alarm bell, I turned and checked the hall. None of the doors seemed to be open, but I was sure that I heard the click of a door shutting. I allowed the elevator door to close, and I leaned against the wall for support. I was still trembling.

I found Uncle Jim waiting in the office. He was seated at my desk, and when I walked in, he tossed the Boulder police report about the theft onto a pile of papers.

"It's my turn to stand watch," I told him. "You can get some dinner now."

"I will in a minute," he said and leaned back in the chair. "Have you read this police report?"

"Yes," I said. "Ramon brought it by this morning."

"Maybe I can help you figure out who stole that check," Uncle Jim said. "Ramon and Morgan have to work on the murder, but we might be able to better protect the check in our safe if we work as a team. First thing to do is figure out what really happened last year."

I hesitated. I began to remind him that I was able to handle everything myself. Then I thought about what Dad and Gran had said about teamwork. Maybe I should stop trying to prove I could do the job without help. I've always been happy when I could help Uncle Jim. In turn, I should be glad to accept his help.

"Thanks," I said. "Did you find anything useful in the police report?"

"A couple of things," Uncle Jim said. "The person who stole the check took it to Duncan Tyler's bank. We don't know if it was on purpose, to make it look as if Tyler had cashed it himself. Or it could have been by accident. The thief was taking a big chance that he'd get a teller who would have recognized the real Duncan Tyler. Also," Uncle Jim added, "the thief had to be male. The bank teller would have been suspicious of a woman cashing a check made out to a Duncan Tyler."

"I'd thought of that too," I said.

"Mark could be our thief," Uncle Jim said. "He told everyone that he and Tyler used to go out drinking together. He probably knew Tyler's lifestyle and habits better than the other writers did."

"Do you really believe Mark when he talks about going to wild parties with Duncan?" I asked.

Uncle Jim laughed. "Mark's a show-off. I don't normally believe much of what a guy like that says. But he did know Duncan pretty well."

"Amy sat at one end of the table at the award dinner last year, and Mark sat at the other end," I said. "I don't see how Mark could have reached the briefcase with the check in it."

I picked up the police report and studied the sketch of where the writers had been seated during the banquet. I pointed it out to Uncle Jim. "I can't figure out how any of them could have taken the check out of the briefcase without being noticed."

Uncle Jim took a close look at the sketch. "Tyler sat next to Amy. Did he know he was going to win the award?"

"Mr. Prescott thinks the writers have a good idea who's going to win," I said. I thought a moment and added, "I've been wondering if Greg and Ginger worked together to steal the check. Greg could have taken the check while Ginger distracted everyone."

"Have you asked if Ginger did anything distracting during the dinner?"

"She threw her arms around Duncan's neck and kissed him," I said.

"That would be distracting, all right," Uncle Jim said. We both laughed.

I went on. "Let's think about this seriously. Ginger distracted everyone. Greg stole the check. Then the next morning Greg took the check to the bank. Ginger could have covered for him if anyone had asked for Greg. He was in the room, or taking a shower—whatever she thought of at the time."

"Where did they hide the check until Greg cashed it in the morning?" Uncle Jim asked. "Their room was searched by the police."

I shrugged. "I don't know. All the writers had their rooms searched. The check couldn't be found."

"Can you see any kind of link between the thief last year and the murderer this year?" Uncle Jim asked.

"Only a couple of guesses. Nothing we could prove," I said.

Just then Gran came into the office. She immediately sent Uncle Jim off to eat dinner. Then she took his chair. "How are you coming with the investigation, dear?" she asked me.

"I'm stuck," I admitted. "But I've thought of some questions that you might be able to answer."

Gran sat forward eagerly. "Go ahead," she said. "What do you want to know?"

"How many of Lady Jane's books have you read?"

Gran smiled. "Every one. I really enjoy them. They take place in a small town in England, but it reminds me of Silver Ridge. The people gossip and worry about each other while the inspector is solving the mystery."

"Do you know much about Lady Jane?"

"Just what it tells about the author on a page in the back of each book." Gran closed her eyes, trying to remember the short biography. She recited, "Lady Jane lives in Denver with her husband and her grown son. She grew up in a village in England where her father raised thoroughbred horses. Now her brother raises them. She's written six books in the series. Frankly, judging from the loving way she describes the village in her stories, I think she's homesick."

That wasn't the answer I had expected, but I had another question. "Lady Jane ordered champagne 'in honor of bright relief.' Do you have any idea what 'bright relief' means?"

Gran looked puzzled. "I have no idea," she answered.

"Could it have come from one of her books? Or could it be the title of a new book?"

"No," Gran said. "All her books have the word *village* in their titles."

I put my head into my hands. "If 'bright relief' isn't the title of a book, then what could it be?" I asked.

"Maybe it's the name of a horse," Gran said. "Lady Jane writes about racehorses in her books, and all the horses have interesting names."

I thought about what Gran was telling me. I began to get excited. "Does Lady Jane own horses?"

Gran perked up. "I can answer that question," she said. "This morning Lady Jane and I had a nice chat about horses. She told me that she hasn't owned a horse since she got married. Her husband travels a great deal in his business, and she likes to travel with him. That lifestyle makes it impossible to raise horses."

I held my breath as the idea grew. Finally I said slowly and carefully, "Does Lady Jane gamble on horses?"

"Yes. She told me that she sometimes visits the racetracks," Gran said. "But she complained that she doesn't often get the chance."

I spoke my thoughts aloud. "She wouldn't have to visit the tracks if she was involved in illegal gambling."

Gran gasped, and I said, "It's a perfect reason for blackmail! Duncan had been blackmailing the authors. They all admitted it. But I never believed Lady Jane's silly story that she was threatened with blackmail because she was out of favor with the Queen. It makes more sense that Duncan threatened blackmail because of Lady Jane's illegal gambling habits."

"How will you find out?" Gran asked.

"I'm not sure," I answered.

"Be careful," Gran said. She took my hand, and I could feel her tremble. I knew what she was thinking. "If Lady Jane murdered Duncan because he knew her secret, she wouldn't hesitate to murder anyone else who discovered it too!"

CHAPTER 14

There was no indirect way to get answers to my questions. I waited just inside Champagne's while Walter Hampton and his mother ate dinner. Finally she patted her lips with her napkin, stood, and left the table. I hurried to join Mr. Hampton before he left too.

"Good evening," I said to him as I slipped into an extra chair at the table. "It's a shame that your mother didn't get to celebrate on Friday night."

"She's pleased about winning the award," he said stiffly.

"Oh, I meant Bright Relief's win. You know—the horse that came in for her."

I watched Mr. Hampton carefully to see how he'd react. I thought he might begin shouting again, but instead he took a sharp breath, then lowered his voice. "How do you know about that?"

"She mentioned it to the bellman who brought her the bottle of champagne she ordered."

Mr. Hampton angrily slapped the table. "It's bad enough that she gambles. But why does she have to tell total strangers when she wins!"

I tried to keep the conversation light and friendly. "Has she run up big gambling debts?" I asked.

"No, she isn't in debt," he said. He sighed. "She just doesn't understand the gaming laws in the United States. She doesn't believe that she's breaking the law."

I was sure that Mr. Hampton was underestimating his mother. I remembered that he had said she didn't know anything about crime, even though she did research on crime for her mystery novels.

"Duncan tried to blackmail your mother because of her gambling. You had to deal with that, didn't you?" I asked.

Mr. Hampton scowled. "He had no right! He should have—" He broke off and struggled to control himself. When he spoke again he was much more calm. "Mother hadn't told me about Duncan's threats. She handled that problem herself."

I gulped. *Handled the problem? Through murder?* "Why did you come to Silver Ridge?" I asked Mr. Hampton.

He looked at me as though I were particularly stupid. "As you know, last year the award check was stolen. Mother thought she had a good chance of winning this year. So I felt that I should look after her—and the check—this time." He folded his arms and frowned at me.

I didn't let his bad temper bother me. "Then why didn't you travel with her and stay at our hotel on Friday night?"

A voice behind me answered the question. "Because he knew his mother would object," Lady Jane snapped. "I don't need a guardian."

As she took her seat at the table, Mr. Hampton said, "Of course you don't need a guardian, Mother. Prescott Publishing didn't take good care of the check last year, so I thought I should be nearby in case there were any problems."

"The problem is that you were nearby when Duncan was killed. Now you're a suspect too," Lady Jane said. She slowly shook her head as she patted her son's hand. "I didn't need you to come. I knew you'd be furious if you found out about the blackmail. So I took care of everything myself."

That's what her son had said. "What do you mean by taking care of everything?" I asked quickly.

Lady Jane gave me a shocked look. I suppose she could tell what I was thinking from the tone of my voice. "I don't mean that I murdered anyone," she said crossly. "When I met with Duncan, I told him that he could go ahead and keep the chapter about my gambling in his book. I didn't care. I refused to give him any money."

Mr. Hampton's face turned a dark, angry red. "Why did you tell him that?" he muttered.

"Because I knew Joshua Prescott would never publish Duncan's book," Lady Jane answered.

"But what if Duncan had been blackmailing Mr. Prescott too?" I asked. I was eager to see her reaction.

Lady Jane just smiled. "Joshua is an honest man. There was nothing Duncan could have used to blackmail him."

Without another word she rose and marched out of the restaurant. Walter followed her. I waited a moment, then headed for the lobby.

In the lobby I ran into Morgan and Ramon. They both looked as tired as I felt. Morgan said, "I'm going home to a very late dinner," and left.

But Ramon and I ate sandwiches in my office while

I told him everything I'd found out.

When we'd finished Ramon eyed my uncomfortable sofa. "Let's sit in the lobby," he suggested.

We sat together on a sofa near the big fireplace. Ramon squirmed as he tried to settle into a comfortable spot. "What's wrong with your sofas?" he asked. "This one is even more uncomfortable than the one in your office."

"Move closer to me," I told him. "It's very comfortable over here."

He put an arm around my shoulders, and I snuggled against him. I tried not to notice Great-grandfather Pierre Champagne staring down at us from the painting hanging over the fireplace.

It was late, and the lobby was quiet. There was only the click of the computer keyboard at the reception desk as Gloria finished the records for the day. Through the large picture window, Ramon and I could see the flowers in the pots that lined the porch, their outlines softened by moonlight. Ramon took my hand in both of his, and I leaned my head against his shoulder. I felt relaxed for the first time in days, and I wanted to forget all the problems of the weekend.

Ramon glanced around the lobby and saw that no one else was on hand, so he kissed me. Then he leaned back. "We need to talk," he said.

I kept myself from groaning aloud. "About the murder?" I asked.

Ramon grinned at me. "Stacy, forget about being Chief of Security for a few minutes. Forget the murder. I want to talk about us."

"What about us?" I snuggled even closer and almost purred.

"Cops make lousy husbands," Ramon said. "Terrible

hours. Stress like you wouldn't believe. It's tough on family life."

I got a cold, tight feeling in the pit of my stomach. "What are you trying to tell me?" I asked.

Before Ramon could answer, the phone rang at the desk. Gloria answered on the first ring and called to Ramon. "Office Morgan wants to talk to you about a report from the lab."

As Ramon walked over to the desk and took the phone, Gloria gave me a smile to show that she was sorry she had to interrupt us. She wasn't as sorry as I was. What had Ramon been going to say?

He hung up the phone, came back, and sat next to me. Unfortunately, he was all business. "Sorry, Stacy," he said. "Morgan's been going over the reports from the lab. He wanted me to have the new information. Do you remember the pile of ashes in the ashtray on the desk in Tyler's room?"

I didn't want to remember. I was still absorbed with what Ramon had been going to say to me. However, he was waiting for my answer, so I tried to be as professional as he was. "Did the lab discover the source of all that ash?" I asked.

"Yes," he said. "There was a very small amount of cigar ash. Most was from paper."

"The manuscript?"

"I don't think so. The lab found some microscopic scraps of paper that hadn't burned. The paper was from a yellow tablet—probably the one on the desk."

I remembered the tablet. "Nothing was written on it," I said. "But something must have been written on the pages that were burned." I remembered when I was young, I could lightly rub a pencil over the top sheet on a pad of paper and bring up words or numbers. "How about indentations on the tablet?" I asked.

"The lab tested it," Ramon said. "Nothing showed up."

I began thinking out loud. "Mark must have burned the pages in the ashtray he brought to Duncan's room. He'd know what had been written."

"I already talked to Mark," Ramon told me. "He said he knew nothing about any pages from the tablet. He had the first appointment. He brought his ashtray but forgot about it and left it on the desk. Any of the writers could have used it to burn the pages."

"Did you ask if any of them remembered a filled ashtray?"

"I did, and none of them remembered what was on the desk. They all explained that they were upset and concerned only about Tyler and his blackmail threats."

"That may be the truth," I admitted.

"Greg did remember that before they had their talk, Tyler offered wine. He gave Ginger a goblet, but Greg had to drink out of a plain water glass. He was angry about it."

"Poor Greg," I said. "Do you think that Duncan did that just to be rude?"

Ramon shrugged. He seemed to be thinking more about the evidence than about Duncan's behavior. "Did I tell you that the legal agreement Ginger told you about turned up with the papers found at the crime scene?"

"Do you mean the agreement that would give Duncan a cut of their income from the perfume company?"

"Yes. It was just one sheet, and it had been tucked into the back of the yellow tablet," Ramon said. "But it wasn't exactly as Ginger had described it. There was only one line to be signed, and that had Greg's name typed under it. There was no place for Ginger to sign."

Ramon pulled out his notebook and wrote a brief message to himself. "I'll ask Ginger more about it."

He frowned at the notebook. Then he held it up for me to see. He had filled the page with questions to ask each of the writers. "Stacy, how am I going to get all of this done?" he asked. "Do you realize that the writers are going to leave tomorrow afternoon?"

"Can't Morgan insist that they stay longer?"

Ramon looked discouraged. "He won't ask them to stay unless we're close to making an arrest, and we don't have the evidence we need to arrest anyone."

I knew too that it would be much harder to investigate the case when all the suspects were out of town. "I'll help with whatever needs to be done," I said. I just hoped it wouldn't be more than I could handle.

CHAPTER
15

Trouble was not what I had expected to find before breakfast on Sunday morning. I woke up, not to the music on my clock radio, but to the phone ringing. Keisha at the front desk had called me, and she sounded unhappy.

"Walter Hampton is here to check out and go back to Denver. He wants to take his mother home, and Mark Bannon wants to go with him. Officer Morgan didn't say that they could leave, and I don't know what to do."

"I'll be right there," I said. "Tell Mr. Hampton that I'll be down in five miniutes. Give him some coffee. *Free* coffee. You can even give him a complimentary cinnamon roll from the coffee shop." Most people don't mind waiting if they can fill the time with coffee and cinnamon rolls.

I phoned Morgan while I pulled my clothes on. The officer who answered the phone told me that Morgan was already on his way to the hotel. Maybe he would arrive in time to keep Mr. Hampton from leaving. I telephoned Ramon next, catching him before he had left for the sheriff's headquarters.

"They can't leave yet," Ramon said. "You saw my notebook, Stacy. I have a lot more questions to ask them." He groaned. "Of course, legally, I can't make them stay."

"I'll do my best to keep them here," I said. But a few seconds later, while I brushed my hair, I knew I needed help. I headed for the third floor, not for the lobby. I knocked at the door of Joshua Prescott's room, hoping he was awake and would talk to me.

Mr. Prescott looked surprised to see me when he opened the door. He squinted, studying my face. "Has something happened, Miss Champagne?"

"Some of the writers want to leave for Denver now," I said.

Mr. Prescott shook his head. "I told them that we're keeping the original schedule. We'll check out at noon, have lunch here, and Amy will drive the van back to Denver." He spoke firmly. He was definitely a man who made up his mind and followed his decisions. I didn't think the writers would argue with him. That was why I had come for his help.

"Walter Hampton wants to take his mother to Denver now," I explained. "And Mark Bannon wants to go with them."

"That's for Walter to decide," Mr. Prescott said stiffly. He began to shut the door.

"Please give me a minute," I said. "If you ask the writers to stay and answer the questions the police have for them, they'll listen to you."

Mr. Prescott gave me a questioning look. "This has been a difficult time. I didn't sleep well last night." He paused. Then he began to speak, but stopped. I could see that he found it hard to tell me what he was thinking. "I can't believe that one of these people—people I've known for years—would commit a murder," he said. "Someone outside our group must have committed this horrible crime."

I pleaded, "If the writers would stay a few more hours and answer more questions, they'd help the police find the guilty person. I need to know who did this."

"What if the murderer turns out to be someone on your staff?"

"Every person on my staff will be a suspect until the truth is known. My staff needs me to find the truth and uncover the killer's identity."

Mr. Prescott sighed. "It doesn't go away, does it? Some people still suspect Amy over that stupid theft of the award check last year. Very well, I'll ask the writers to stay. I'll be able to come downstairs in about fifteen minutes."

He looked so unhappy, I wished I could comfort him. But he obviously didn't want to talk to me any longer.

The elevator doors opened the moment I pressed the button. As I rode down to the first floor, I realized I hadn't felt creepy on the third floor, the way I had when I thought I was being watched. Was it because the watcher wasn't on hand?

Mark, Walter Hampton, and Lady Jane were waiting for me in the lobby. Mark sat on the sofa Ramon had chosen last night. Mark leaned back, took another sip of coffee, and smiled at me. Lady Jane sat across from him in one of a pair of blue-striped, upholstered chairs, Mr. Hampton in the other. Mr. Hampton stood up when he saw me. "I resent the delay you've caused," he grumbled.

I didn't take his complaint too seriously, because he was still chewing on a cinnamon roll. "I'm sorry I took so long," I said. "I talked to Mr. Prescott a few minutes ago. He'll be down soon. He asked that you stay and help the police solve this crime."

Walter snapped, "I don't care what Mr. Prescott said."

His mother interrupted. "I do." She turned to me. "Is Mr. Prescott going to stay here through lunch as we had planned?"

"Yes," I answered.

Lady Jane put a hand on Walter's arm. "Sit down, dear. I think we should stay. Besides helping the police, I have an idea for a new series that I'd like to discuss with Joshua."

"You won't have time to talk business if you're answering questions for the police," Walter insisted.

Mark leaned forward and put his cup on the low coffee table. "Don't you want to get out of this place, Lady Jane?" he asked. "This weekend has been anything but a restful vacation retreat. We've already done all we can to help the police."

I was quick to disagree with him. "There are still questions you could answer."

Mark shrugged. "I've told the police all that I know."

"I don't think so," Lady Jane said. "You spent more time with Duncan than the rest of us, Mark. You could tell the police quite a bit about the nightspots Duncan visited and the people he knew."

Mark shifted nervously and looked away. "That's private information. I don't want to talk about it."

Lady Jane was not impressed. "Why not? Duncan was willing to tell all in his book."

"I don't think so," Mark said. "Duncan had to have been joking about what he claimed to have written. I'm surprised that you took him seriously."

"He seemed serious enough to me," she said.

I watched Mr. Hampton's face. Had he also taken Duncan seriously? Had he come to Duncan's hotel room and argued with him on Friday evening?

Mr. Hampton didn't show what he was thinking. He turned and looked out the window, watching Officer Morgan march up the walk to the hotel. I noticed that Morgan's shoulders looked tense. I'm sure he wanted to have this murder solved before the writers left Silver Ridge.

Mark kept arguing with Lady Jane. "I helped all I could. I even allowed the police to search my room. Now we should all take care of ourselves and go back to Denver."

Lady Jane set her coffee cup on the table. "No. I want a chance to talk with Joshua."

"This isn't the time or the place. He isn't going to want to think about story lines now. You're just fooling yourself," Mark said crossly.

Lady Jane tilted her head and seemed to be thinking about what he had said. Finally she answered, "Life must go on, Mark. Joshua knows that. He's a successful businessman. He'll listen to my ideas."

Mark angrily slapped the arm of the sofa. Then he smiled and turned to Walter. "Okay, let her stay here. You and I could still go to Denver. I'll buy you a drink. I know some great places."

I could hear the disgust in Mr. Hampton's voice. "Don't be silly. My only reason for being here is to help my mother."

"That's not fair. How about me?" Mark complained.

Morgan entered the hotel and walked briskly toward us. "I understand that some of you want to leave Silver Ridge this morning," he began.

Lady Jane shook her head. "We've changed our minds," she said.

But Mark pouted. "We'd leave if we had transportation," he mumbled.

"Since you don't, suppose you answer a few questions for me," Morgan said. "Mr. Bannon, I'd like to know more about the time you spent with Tyler. Were there certain places you visited regularly?"

"I don't want to talk about it," Mark said.

Morgan took a huge breath, and I could see he was trying to be patient. "Maybe so," he said, "but I need you to give me some answers. Did you go to the same nightspots regularly, or did you visit different places?"

"Different places," Mark said. He folded his arms and leaned back against the sofa.

"Let's talk about this last month," Morgan said. "Give me some names."

Reluctantly Mark said, "Okay. Two weeks ago we went to a British pub and had a few drinks and met a couple of friendly young women."

"Oh, for goodness sakes!" Lady Jane put in. "That wasn't a night on the town. It was a program for writers about interesting murder cases that took place in Great Britain. Only it wasn't interesting. The speaker was boring."

Mark frowned at her. "I didn't say it was a wild party. I tried to answer the question about what Duncan and I did last month."

"Have you ever really been to a wild party?" Lady Jane asked.

"I wouldn't talk about it in front of you," Mark said. He caught me watching him and winked broadly. "Or in front of this sweet young lady. She's dating the deputy sheriff, and I don't want to get arrested for shocking her."

Sweet young lady? As our hotel's Chief of Security, I was furious. I clenched my fists and felt my face grow hot. But Morgan threw me a warning look, so I stomped away to cool down. Besides, I didn't think that Mark was going to admit anything shocking. Morgan didn't seem to be getting him to admit anything at all. I saw Ramon arriving, so I met him at the front door.

"We don't have much time," Ramon said quickly. "Is there any place we've overlooked in our search for the manuscript?"

I shook my head. My search in the hotel had been a failure. I'd gone over every possible spot on all four floors, remembering all my favorite hiding places. But I hadn't included Walter Hampton's activities in my search. If he had been the one who took the manuscript, he could have gotten rid of it at the Mountain Motel Friday night. By now, his room would have been cleaned and rented again. If the manuscript had been there, Elena would have found it and called Officer Morgan. Even so, I wanted to check every detail. While Ramon left to join Morgan, I phoned Elena.

"I'm sorry, but nothing like that has turned up," Elena said. "I hope Mr. Hampton isn't adding to your troubles. He complained about one thing after another the whole time he was here."

"He had a few complaints here too," I told her.

Elena giggled, "He was upset because we don't have a restaurant, and he didn't want to go out to eat. I couldn't build him a restaurant right on the spot, so I talked him into ordering a pizza. Then he sat in the lobby and complained because it took so long to get here. The delivery guy didn't show up until after seven."

I was startled. "Tell me that again! Are you saying Mr. Hampton was in the lobby fussing at you around seven on Friday night? Are you sure about the time?" If Walter Hampton was in the lobby of Mountain Motel with Elena at seven, he couldn't be the person Lew saw leaving Duncan Tyler's room.

Elena laughed at my question. "Stacy, you know I've got three clocks in the lobby. Mr. Hampton came down to the desk just before six-thirty. I couldn't get rid of him until after he got his pizza, and that was a couple of minutes after seven."

"So he left at seven o'clock." I tried to figure out if there was some way he could have reached our hotel and murdered Duncan.

"Yes," Elena said, "but five minutes later, he phoned from his room. He couldn't get his television to work. It wasn't a big problem. The remote control just needed new batteries. I fixed it in a minute, but that wasn't the end of his complaints. He phoned me twice more before nine to complain about the mattress being too hard and about someone being noisy in the hall."

After I finished my conversation with Elena, I thought about what she had told me. If Walter Hampton had been at the Mountain Motel causing problems for Elena, he couldn't have been here at the Silver Ridge. There was no way he could have murdered Duncan around seven.

Then I began to wonder. Could Mr. Hampton have killed Duncan earlier in the evening? Could the visitor Lew saw have been quietly leaving because he had found Duncan already dead? Were we putting too much faith in the timetable Duncan had written?

Where were we going to find the answers?

CHAPTER 16

I glanced at the clock. It was already ten-thirty. In a few minutes the writers would be checking out, and I'd need to help bring their baggage downstairs. Was my new idea important? Would I have enough time to figure out the answer? I thumbed through the papers on my desk until I found the copy of the timetable from Duncan's desk.

The schedule was typed on a plain sheet of paper. There was only the list of writers' names and the times of their appointments. Mark had been first, and he had left his ashtray on Duncan's desk. Next Clara had come, and she'd paid Duncan the blackmail money he'd wanted. Then Lady Jane had met with Duncan. Greg and Ginger had been last. Lew Parker had seen a single person leave Duncan's room at seven. Who was that? Ginger? Or Greg? And wouldn't they both be arriving, not leaving?

What if the schedule was wrong? I stared at the paper in front of me. Duncan didn't have a computer with him, so he must have printed this schedule before he got to the hotel. He couldn't have been sure that the other writers would be on time or even remember when they were supposed to meet him. Should we depend on this timetable?

Now that I was asking questions about the timetable, I saw another problem with it. Why did Duncan meet with Greg and Ginger at the same time? He was blackmailing Greg over the forged check he wrote in college, but he was blackmailing Ginger over her romance with him—something she wouldn't want Greg to know about. Ginger had told me that she and Greg had received separate letters from Duncan. Why did he send two letters, then plan a meeting with both Greg and Ginger at the same time? I began to get excited. All the loose pieces of the puzzle were coming together and making sense.

I knew now why Duncan had been so bad tempered. Duncan hadn't expected Greg to visit him at the same time as Ginger. She had surprised him by bringing Greg with her. Yet, there was their appointment on the schedule—at the same time.

The paper shook in my hands as I realized this timetable was a fake! Duncan hadn't typed it because he had set up a different schedule. Someone else had called Ginger to tell her to come with Greg at six. And the caller had brought this fake schedule to the hotel!

There was a knock at the office door. Lady Jane pushed open the door and came into the room. "I'd like my award check, please," she said.

Last Friday afternoon I had thought my biggest problem would be guarding the award. How wrong I had been! I opened the safe and removed the envelope. The mark I had made on it was still there. No one had switched envelopes.

I watched carefully as Lady Jane opened the envelope and pulled out the check. She signed the receipt, and I gave a sigh of relief. At least I'd accomplished one thing. I'd kept the check from being stolen.

Lady Jane had another request. "Can you have someone bring down my luggage and Walter's? We'll check out at eleven."

Lew wouldn't return to work for a few more days, so I said, "Yes. I'll take care of it myself." I added politely, "Did you get a chance to tell Mr. Prescott your idea for a new series?"

"I did, and he likes the idea." Lady Jane leaned over the desk and lowered her voice. "I had another reason for wanting to stay later. I didn't want to ride back to Denver with Mark. I don't know why Walter offered to take him with us. Now Mark can ride in the van with the others."

"Why did you want to avoid the trip with Mark?" I asked.

"Last year he told us he gets carsick. He insisted on sitting right behind Amy during the drive," Lady Jane said. "He made a real nuisance out of himself."

Here was a chance to check out my idea about the fake timetable. "Lady Jane, would you mind telling me again what time you met with Duncan?"

She nodded pleasantly. "A little after six-thirty, but I only stayed a few minutes. It didn't take long to tell him I wouldn't pay blackmail."

"Had there been a change in time? Or was this the same time Duncan had asked to meet with you in the letter you received?"

"It was the same time," Lady Jane said. "Duncan checked my name off on the schedule he'd written on the yellow tablet."

I nearly dropped the pen in my hand. "On the yellow tablet?" I repeated. "Did you see the entire timetable? Can you remember it?"

Lady Jane thought a moment, then slowly shook her head. "I didn't pay that much attention. It didn't interest me."

I didn't give up. I tried to keep my voice calm so that Lady Jane wouldn't realize the importance of my next question. "Do you remember if there was one name or two for the appointment after yours?" I asked.

"I think there was just one other name after mine," she answered. "I can't give you a definite answer, because I was busy telling Duncan what I thought of him."

Lady Jane tucked the envelope with the check in it into her purse. She stood up. "I should see if Walter is ready. Don't forget our luggage. Oh, and thank you for taking care of the award."

She left my office, but my mind was whirling with the information she had given me. Duncan's timetable was written on the yellow tablet. No wonder the police hadn't found the timetable. That's what had been burned in the ashtray. After Duncan's death, the printed timetable had been left on his desk.

I was shocked. Duncan's murder hadn't been a sudden act of anger. It had been planned. Someone had known the times of the various appointments and had printed out this schedule even before the writers' weekend began.

Had all the writers discussed the meetings by telephone in advance? Or had one of them had access to Duncan's office?

We knew that Clara had telephoned Ginger. I remembered the look of pain on Clara's face when she told us that Duncan had ruined her life. Had she been frightened enough to plan his murder?

Lady Jane seemed to have known what Duncan was up to. She wasn't upset for herself, but she was well aware of her son's desperate need to protect both his and her reputations. She doted on her son. How far would she have gone to protect him?

Mark bragged about being buddy-buddy with Duncan. They went to nightspots together. Since they were friends, it seemed logical that they'd have visited each other's homes. Could Mark have seen Duncan's schedule of visitors and copied it?

Greg and Ginger were a team, both of them clever enough to plot a murder on paper. I had no trouble imagining them planning a real murder in an attempt to save a business deal that could make them wealthy.

The telephone rang, and I answered. "The Prescotts are checking out but staying for lunch," Keisha said. "Is that okay?"

I looked at the clock. It was exactly eleven-thirty. I was running out of time.

"Do you know where Morgan or Ramon are now?" I asked.

"On the third floor, I think," she said. "They wanted to talk to the Gages."

I had business on the third floor too. I took a luggage cart with me and knocked on the door of Lady Jane's room.

As she opened the door, she said, "Walter brought his bags to my room, and you can take them, but I'm not quite ready yet. I need to clean my contact lenses."

"I'll take the rest of your luggage," I said. I loaded it and went to Mr. Prescott's room. Amy had joined him and had brought her suitcase and briefcase with her. I added their luggage to the cart and rolled it out into the hallway.

"Before we go downstairs, may I ask you a few more questions?" I said to both Prescotts.

"Of course," Amy said, and her grandfather nodded agreement.

"The printed envelope you used for the award," I said to Amy. "Do you keep those envelopes in your office?"

She looked surprised. "Yes," she answered. "I have a drawer in my desk with the company's letterhead and envelopes. That way, they're nearby when I need them."

"Was it the same way last year?"

"Yes."

I had one more question, "Do you keep your desk locked?"

"Oh, yes," she said. "I lock it every evening before I leave the office." She looked startled as if she knew what I'd ask next. "But not during the day while I'm at work. There's no need to lock it then."

"Thanks," I said. I pushed my cart to the elevators and pressed the button.

When we arrived at the lobby level, I rolled the luggage cart over to the bell station. My mind wasn't on the luggage. I was too busy trying to figure out how the check had been stolen last year. I was sure now that it had been stolen long before the award dinner took place.

I suspected that Mark had taken the check, and he had used a simple plan. While he was in Amy's office, he had told her he got carsick. He'd asked her to get him some medicine for motion sickness. While she was gone from her office, Mark took an empty envelope and a sheet of paper from her desk and pocketed them. Then Mark insisted on riding just behind Amy in the van. While Amy was busy driving and the other writers weren't paying attention, Mark had traded the stolen envelope, with a folded paper inside it, for the envelope containing the check. That had been the easiest part.

Mark would have had to hide the award check until he could take it to Duncan's bank and cash it. That's why Mark had left his shaving kit in the van. He must have hidden the check in it. The police could search his hotel room, but they wouldn't find the check. They wouldn't see a need to search the van. It had been parked and locked since the writers had arrived. On Saturday morning, Mark could ask Amy to get his shaving kit from the van. Then he could go to Duncan's bank and cash the check.

I couldn't prove any of this. I didn't have any evidence, but this made more sense to me than anything else we'd thought about. I felt sure I was right.

Maybe Duncan had figured all this out too. Maybe that's why he was blackmailing Mark. But why blackmail instead of demanding to be given the amount on the check? That wasn't too hard to figure out. The amount Duncan asked to be paid must have been a great deal higher than the amount of the check.

I needed to talk to Ramon and tell him what I was thinking.

I glanced at the sofa where Ramon and I had been sitting the evening before. One of the seat cushions was jutting out, and its cover seemed to be twisted. I picked it up to straighten it and saw that the zipper at the back was open. I pushed and pulled until the cover fit snugly. Then I closed the zipper.

I saw Keisha watching me, so I walked over to the desk. "What happened to the sofa cushion?" I asked.

Keisha shrugged. "I don't know. Early this morning, Mark Bannon was sitting there. He's a strange guy. He asked me to get him a cup of coffee, so I did. But when I brought it to him he didn't drink it."

"He sent you out of the room," I said.

"Well, sure," Keisha answered. "Where else would I get coffee? It was early—before the coffee shop opened—when he asked me, so I went to the kitchen to get it.

I began thinking about the way Mark had hidden last year's check. What would he be hiding this year? It had to have been the manuscript.

Mark couldn't have shoved the manuscript pages into the

sofa on Friday evening. There were too many people in the lobby. Someone would have seen him. If Mark had been the person Lew saw leaving Duncan's room, then Mark would have come down the stairs with the manuscript. How did Mark carry it over to the sofa without being seen?

I studied the door that led to the stairs. Anyone coming through that door would be next to the hallway that led to the ballroom and the meeting rooms. I thought about the large vase that had struck Lew. Had Mark hidden the manuscript under the artificial flowers inside the vase?

On Friday afternoon he could have walked through the first floor of the hotel, looking it over and planning a hiding place for the manuscript. No one would have thought he was anything other than a curious guest.

Was Mark afraid that Lew would remember more about the person he saw leaving Duncan's room? Did he send word to Lew to go to the ballroom? Did he step up behind Lew and hit him hard to enough to kill him? I shuddered, thankful that the blow hadn't been that strong.

Once he had broken the vase over Lew's head, Mark would have needed a new hiding place for the manuscript. He must have stuffed the pages inside the sofa cushion in a hurry. They had been there all during the police search.

Mark couldn't leave the manuscript in the hotel. He had to take it with him. That was easy. While Keisha was getting his coffee, he'd removed the manuscript from the cushion and put it into his suitcase, which was next to him. His things had already been searched. No one would look in his suitcase again before he left.

The coat worried me. Did Mark bring a coat? If he did, would he have tried to get rid of it? I thought I knew where it might be.

I saw Mark's suitcase with the others stacked by the bell stand. I looked around the lobby, but Mark wasn't in sight. I needed to find Ramon. "Keisha," I said, "will you please call the Gages' room and see if Ramon is still there? Tell him I'll meet him on the third floor. And will you ask Morgan to check the lost and found closet for a man's dark coat?"

Keisha began dialing as I headed toward the elevators.

I had to wait for an elevator, and it seemed to take forever before it reached the third floor.

The door opened, and I stepped forward, but Mark Bannon, red-faced and out of breath, jumped inside the elevator, blocking my way. He hit the button to close the door, then punched the fourth floor button.

"Earlier, I was looking around the hotel," he managed to say between raspy breaths. "There's a door leading to the roof on the fourth floor."

I could see what he had in mind, and I was so scared I shivered. "That door's locked," I said quickly.

"No, it's not." Mark grinned. He put a hand over his chest and took a deep breath. "Running up those stairs to meet your elevator was harder than I thought."

I tried to stay calm. "Let's go down to the lobby," I said. "Let's talk to Morgan or Ramon."

"No more questions and answers," Mark said. "You talk too much as it is. I could tell from what you said to Keisha after you zipped up the sofa cushion that you'd figured everything out."

"You were watching me?"

His grin widened. "Sure. I had to protect myself. I've been watching you ever since I found out that you were the one Lew told what he saw."

The bell rang, and the door opened on the fourth floor. Mark grabbed my arm and tugged me toward the door, but I fought back. I clutched the rail at the back of the elevator and held on tightly. Mark grunted and tried to jerk me loose. I stomped on his foot.

The door of the elevator began to close. Mark let go of me with one hand and punched at the button again. Then he gave a frantic tug, and my grip on the rail broke. We tumbled against the elevator doors, but they had closed. The elevator was headed down.

I tried to stand up, but Mark was trying to stand too, and we fell over each other. I tried to reach the alarm, but Mark pulled my arm down. I swung my hand forward and managed to hit the button for the third floor.

As Mark twisted my arm behind me, I kicked his knee. He moaned, but he didn't release his hold on me.

The elevator door opened, and I struggled to get out, but Mark tugged me back.

Suddenly someone flew past me. Mark made a strangled sound and let go of me. I rolled into the hallway, sat up, and turned to see what had happened.

Mark was lying face down with Ramon snapping handcuffs on him.

As the door began to close, Morgan shoved past me. He traded places with Ramon and I heard him begin to read Mark his rights.

Ramon knelt on the hall floor next to me. "Are you okay, Stacy?" he asked.

"I'm fine," I said quickly. There were more important things to talk about. "I think I know where the manuscript is! It's in Mark's suitcase!" I told Ramon what I'd worked out, and he smiled broadly.

"You're the best Chief of Security I've ever met," he said.

I brushed down my skirt and tried to stand. "We'd better hurry down and help Morgan."

Ramon shook his head and wrapped his arms around me. "Morgan doesn't need our help."

"But—"

"We have to finish the conversation we were having last night," Ramon said. "Do you remember what we were talking about?"

I nodded. "You said something very negative about cops making bad husbands."

"I didn't mean to be negative," Ramon said. "I just wanted you to know what you'd be getting into if we got married."

My heart gave a bounce. "Married? You were asking me to marry you?"

"I guess I'm not very good at proposals," Ramon said.

He looked so dejected, I reached up and took his face between my hands. "But you got what you asked for," I told him. "The answer is yes. Everyone keeps telling me that teamwork is important, and I think they're right." As my lips met Ramon's, I murmured, "You and I are going to make a great team!"